HIDDEN SHAME

HIDDEN SHAME

Hidden Justice Book Three

NOLON KING

DAVID W. WRIGHT

STERLING & STONE

To YOU, the reader.
Thank you for your support.
Thank you for the wonderful emails.
Thank you for the thoughtful reviews.
Thank you for reading and loving our stories.

Chapter One

THE WORLD KNOWS how to cover up a crime. The creep of nature. The crawl of time.

In a secluded marsh, where the drowned weeds and fallen leaves sink to the bottom. To belch up their decomposition, making the black water bubble and gurgle like the final breaths of a dying chorus.

In the distance is the faint beckoning whisper of passing traffic. Rushing by like the life of an ant to a plodding rhinoceros. The world can't understand the hurry.

The rushing intent of the beings crawling across her surface. Making every short second count. For the world, time is measured in ages.

Not enough has yet passed to cover up this crime, but the world is patient.

Faint lines in the ground. Twin trails winding through the thick vegetation, covered in reaching vines and hanging grasses. They lead into the murky shadow of the water's edge. Where the ground sinks down to form the choked shoreline.

To a wall of climbing tendrils too straight to have

formed by nature. Spreading up and over a layer of greasy algae. Tufts of moss. Black trails of waste and grit.

The wall of spreading vegetation forms around an unnatural shape. The back of a van angled out of the water.

The flaking white paint showing through the vines where they thin at the top. Red rust the same color as the veins and accents in the leaves.

The descent along the ridged roof ends in a heavy line of sediment where the water has risen and fallen with the rains. The drooping canopy of leaves drips a steady beat on the sagging metal.

An arrow of disturbance rolls by on the water's surface. Some large creature making a shallow pass. Back to the scene. Looking for anything that might be left.

To a floating mound of tatters and growth. Swollen with the intrusion of seeking roots, the mass bobs up and down as the creature circles around for another look.

The glint of bone in the scatter of sunlight dancing through the swaying branches above. A skull. Cracked and broken and empty.

Malick Briar no longer exists for the world. Not as anything more than a scaffolding for the expansion of the reserve's growth. Food for the critters living inside it. A home for waterborne insects, mold, and moss.

Yet to those living outside of the world's influence in this place, Malick Briar is real. As a memory. As pain.

Frank Grimm found a man living as a monster. An abuser that could have been the one that raped and murdered his daughter. Jenny Grimm.

And another girl just like her. Rory Day.

And many others, their names and numbers unknown.

Frank focused his every effort on finding this man, then killed him once he did. He and his friends dumped the body into the fetid waters behind his cousin's gym. Along with the van. After the sun set, and before the rain came.

But two of those men weren't his friends after all. They had manipulated Frank into committing this crime. All while being the *real* monsters. Evidence in the back of their car showing *they* were the ones responsible for Rory's rape and murder.

But still not his daughter's ...

Detectives Owens and West. Partners. But when their heinous act was discovered, one turned on the other, and Frank's final hope of finding Jenny's killer died when Owens shot West in the face.

The world has no shame. She exists through time. Doesn't make mistakes. Wouldn't recognize one anyway. But every day, as she continues to exist — to pass another age — she covers the errors of the men and women who spend their lives pushing her away. Driven by their vanity and disgrace.

Frank's triumph was removing the monster. His shame was removing the wrong one. His *crime*. But nobody will know, because the world knows how to cover it up.

Chapter Two

FRANK WONDERED what life would be like if his wife and daughter were still alive. By his side here on the beach.

Not as he had been before their deaths, but as he was now. The man he had become. Frank often wondered what they would have thought of him.

He suspected they wouldn't like him all that much.

The sun beat on the token skim of sunscreen he'd wiped on his shoulders. The generous layer on his scalp. After shaving his head as part of a lifetime disguise, Frank quickly learned what the sun could do to skin that had only ever seen the light through a protective cover of hair. Even hair that had been thinning severely like his.

His white linen shirt was off and tucked into his waistband like a quarterback's towel. Khaki cargo shorts flapped with the warm breeze coming off the ocean.

This far away from the inland marsh kept the air fresh. Free of the usually pungent odor of rotting algae and wet vegetation. And the sand was soft enough to walk barefoot. A hundred yards toward land, and the beach rose into dunes full of gravel and razor-sharp silica particles that would render the bottoms of feet into bleeding slivers.

Layer after layer brought up by the bubbling waters of Playa Dolor.

Frank sneered when he thought of the beach's name. Stan had explained its meaning — Pain Beach. Somebody thought they were being cute. Puns and desperate cleverness had never been high on his list of comedy, even though Frank had engaged in enough of it for Jenny's sake to turn him full hypocrite. Add in his newfound *grumpy old man* persona, and the name made him cringe whenever he heard it.

Playa Dolor.

Named for the marsh full of neurotoxic algae that posed no problem, so long as it never entered your bloodstream. But with an entire beach making bloody mulch out of feet ... you get a natural one-two punch.

The place attracted three kinds of people. Isolationist types. Leave me alone and stay away from me and let me live in peace in this place that protects me from trespassers by virtue of killing the careless that dare enter uninvited.

Thrill-seeking types: *Let me feel like I'm living dangerously by exposing myself to minimal threat as long as I follow the rules laid down by the land itself.*

Science types. And *those* could be broken down into two further groups. Young students and scientists keen on studying the natural compounds found in the algal blooms, and capitalists looking to cash in on said compounds if they were found to be beneficial in *any* capacity.

One of their first conversations about it had seen Stan behaving even more skeptical than usual. Recovering from a gunshot wound to the right trapezius muscle had kept him in a bad mood.

"I tell you what," he had said between big bites of

grilled salmon. "You wait until one of these kids finds some molecule that makes dicks get rock hard, and this place will be fucking *packed* with pharmaceutical assholes."

Frank nodded as if he agreed completely. Then held up a finger to make his point. "But what if they find something that cures cancer?"

Stan had shrugged. "Same thing, I guess. There's just more money in dick stuff."

Cynical discussions like that had become their primary form of communication. It turned exhausting almost at once.

Frank paused to squint into the sun now bouncing off the water. Seaweed reaching up from the mucky bottom. Lying in drying clumps and stinking piles. Brittle strands crunching underfoot.

Even though all the three types of people were separated from each other — by choice or circumstances — they all ended up wanting the same thing after enough time. Others.

Company. A friendly smile and a wave and a quick conversation held over the backyard fence. There was something about the danger and isolation of Playa Dolor that made the inhabitants want to seek out some kind of validation. Hey, I survived and *you* survived. We did it on our own, but we're still in this together. Now get outta my yard.

Frank rarely saw anybody out here. Was forced to admit that Stan had planned for this possibility with a stellar result. It seemed like the perfect place to hide. South of Tallahassee on a secluded beach with the deterrent of natural hostility, and a price tag to keep it exclusive.

Something Frank had never asked about, but something that preyed on his ego. Stan paying for everything in spite of losing everything else. Neither mentioned it, and

Frank wasn't ready to find out where the money came from. Maybe a conversation for another day.

Or, he could die while solving the case. By losing his life he'd no longer be a burden.

He smiled to himself. These flights of morbidity were less frequent than they had been, but Frank could still surprise himself with a bout of dramatic melancholy.

At first, he had stayed inside. Staring into the dark every night. Wondering where he had gone wrong — knowing the answer was his stubborn pride.

Hiding behind the curtains even though he had shaved his head and let his beard grow in.

Almost four weeks he had lived like that while hovering over Stan like a worried hen. Following behind to pick up after him. Arranging his pillows. Asking if there had been any contact with Gen and Mo. If there was any word on GG.

When was Ian going to come out with new phones and internet access? When could he contact Freya and Irene to see if they were okay? When could he get back into the investigation that had led them here?

Finally — over a dinner of grilled chicken and asparagus that Frank was proud of for not burning — Stan had exploded in frustration. "Jesus fuck, Frank! I'm *fine*. Why don't you take care of your *own* shit for a while. Get your fucking head on right, stop drinking so goddamned much, and get some sun, you pasty moth-erfucker!"

Frank had stormed away. To his room where he doffed his shirt and switched his sneakers for flip-flops. Knowing that Stan just didn't understand what he was going through.

He had looked up at his reflection, and froze in shock at the sight of a stranger. Gleaming scalp. Shaggy beard white from temples to chin except for a dark stripe on either side of his mouth. Like a reverse skunk.

Pale skin tight over a torso that hadn't been this lean since running to lose weight for wrestling back in college. Forever ago.

Thick curls of chest hair turned the color of ash while he wasn't looking.

A solid tan line around his noticeable biceps. Dark and leathery forearms. Smooth, pasty skin across his ribs.

Frank didn't recognize the muscle he had gained. The fat he had lost. The stoop in his shoulders. But mostly, he didn't recognize the face. It wasn't the wrinkles and the lines. The white beard and mustache. The veins standing out on the side of his reddening head.

It was the *defeat* that seemed so unfamiliar. The bitter self-pity. Even under the hair, Frank would have known himself, except for the expression of despair twisting his features. Something he had never seen before.

Frank had become a different person without realizing it, and now he saw panic when he looked into his own eyes. What if he was lost to himself forever? What if he could never get back to the man he was?

His head fell as he left the room, knowing he could *never* go back.

Frank left out the front. Down the creaking boardwalk of washed-out planks leading to the safe part of the beach. He emerged out from under the trees into the sun and forced himself to straighten. Raised his shoulders — took a deep breath tainted by the constant funk of marsh behind him — and decided to be a different man. Not a *better* man — just a *different* one — only this time, he would do it on purpose.

He had kicked his flip-flops off. Warmed up with a jog to the ocean. Then a round of sprints that chewed on his feet. But once done, in spite of the throbbing skin on his soles, and the burning skin on his scalp, Frank felt better.

He had avoided Stan for the next two weeks, joining him only for meals. Morning coffee in awkward near-silence.

Frank had turned his maggoty pale skin into a nice even tan. Trimmed his beard to a dignified point. Kept up the sprints, and every morning, saw a little more of that man he wanted to become in the mirror's reflection.

The bloody feet and neurotoxic algae and skin cancer threat from the constant sun barely registered. Much like his fantasy of getting killed by the cops after murdering Malick Briar, Frank accepted this new potential death as something that wouldn't matter once Bryan Owens was dead. He wouldn't be *allowed* to live after exposing the underage sex trafficking business, reaching its talons high into the Florida law enforcement community.

Frank would die when the cops found him standing over Owens' body. Or in prison — if it ever went to trial. They had sent a message to the rapists. Made Malick Briar the wind that swept the storm back toward the open ocean.

It would come back eventually, but for now … he was strangely satisfied with waiting.

Like Stan said, Frank would get his mind right. Keep his body ready. And when the time came, keep the promise he made to his daughter so long ago. A promise meant for *him*.

He would find and kill the man that raped and murdered her.

Frank smiled as he headed back to the boardwalk that lead into the darkness of the marsh. The reflection of the sun glinting off the cabin windows made it look like someone was watching him from the shadows.

Chapter Three

STAN WAS LEARNING how to cook. Or as he would say, "In point of fact, I'm trying to learn how to cook *better*. I already know how to cook. I'm not a fucking idiot."

Frank neither confirmed nor denied that sentiment, and Stan continued to pretend he knew just what he was doing.

The messes had only gotten worse the more he healed.

Bringing his old Wild One mentality to the beach, Stan spent a lot of his days in the sun. Sweating out his frustration on a cardio circuit that left him sweating and gasping and lobster red.

Then a trip into town to eat at Right Sanchez, a drive-thru Mexican joint with an insane portion-to-cost ratio, and flan milkshakes. Evenings spent in idle internet surfing — the only kind they *could* do until Ian came through with a more secure version. Watching cooking videos on Live-Lyfe under a fake account Stan had made.

They were hiding out as a married couple. An old queen named Wendall Scott, and his young stud husband, Trevor. Their social media accounts were owned by these respective identities, and Frank was having fun posting as Wendall.

Pictures of flowers and birds. Stan — *Trevor* — posted nothing but pictures of ill-prepared food. Beverages with sweat rolling down the glass. The sunset view from the porch.

"Should we really be doing this?" Frank had asked.

Stan shrugged. "These dudes have to be real. But *real* life doesn't make *anything* real. The only thing people accept as reality anymore is what they see online. I'm just a nice young gay man helping my darling husband live out his autumn years in relative paradise. Nobody will look past that shit, because it's what they expect."

"People expect nothing but gay couples on the internet?"

"No, sweetie." Stan chuckled. "They expect the veneer. The glossy life people share with the virtual world. If they see what they expect, they won't look any deeper."

They met a neighbor couple and Frank finally understood what Stan had been trying to tell him.

Barney and Melody Hollander. Well into their retirement. Sunny smiles and hunched shoulders. Shuffling steps with plenty of life left in them for a dance or two.

He and Stan had been bickering over the grill. Bluetooth thermometers speared into the steaks didn't seem to be working properly, and Stan was getting frustrated. "How come shit just doesn't work like it's supposed to?" He glared at his phone as if accusing it of murder. "Just fucking *work*!"

"Why do you even need that?" Frank shook his head. "People have been cooking meat since they invented fire."

Stan lowered his hands in defeat. "I'm trying to systematize the process. Remove variables."

Frank stepped over to put their shoulders together.

Motioned for Stan to lift the phone back up so he could take a look. "You can only remove variables you can control."

Stan joined Frank in looking at the app that was supposed to monitor the internal temperature of the steaks. "That's what I'm trying to do, old man."

Frank nodded. "Well, according to this old man, the app says the sensors aren't connected."

"What?" Stan pulled the phone closer to his face and snarled in disgust. "The fucking Bluetooth is on, though. What the fuck?"

Frank threw him a small hug. Gently squeezing his arm across his shoulders. "Let me know if you need any more help. Technology can be challenging."

Stan stared murder at him from the corner of his eye before rolling out from under Frank's arm. Swiping and typing on his phone.

"Ho neighbor!" a voice had shouted from behind him.

Frank spun around, heart in his throat and hand going to the pistol clipped to his belt at the small of his back. Relaxing only after he saw the withered couple coming up the gravel walk. He pasted a welcoming smile on his unwilling lips.

The back of the house faced a gravel lane that connected all the houses in the "neighborhood." He rarely saw more traffic than the mailman, and he and Stan had yet to *get* any mail.

The man wore white shorts under a T-shirt with an American flag. His bald head glistened with sweat, skin red from heat and exertion. He dragged a cooler on wheels behind him. Bouncing and scraping through the rocks.

The woman following him could have been his twin. The same posture and expression. White shorts and whiter tee. She held a casserole dish out in front of her like an offering.

They made themselves immediately comfortable on the patio couch Stan had pushed against the cabin to make room for the giant grill he still didn't know how to use.

Melody handed over the dish — gluten-free vegan brownies — and Barney flipped the lid of his cooler and dug into the ice for a matching set of Coronas. Handed one over to Frank without a request sent either way. Pulled a bottle opener from a loop of chain around his neck.

Stan and Frank had decided their fake histories should be as close to reality as possible. Retired police officer. Injured military veteran. An unlikely romance and a quick marriage. Now living as far away from the bigots as they could get.

Barney had waved his hand in front of his face like shooing a fly. "Don't worry about me and Mel. Whether it dangles or not, or what you do with it don't matter a tick to us."

Melody had raised her beer with an emphatic grin. "Exactly! Besides, you two are adorable together. I can see the love you have for each other, and it's beautiful."

She seemed unsteady in her seat, and by the looks of her red cheeks and nose, this was definitely not her first beer of the day.

Stan and Frank shared a look. Stan batted his eyelashes, and Frank choked on laughter. Covered it up by returning the toast, but the old couple didn't seem to notice.

In fact, Stan and Frank could have made up anything about their pasts, because Barney and Melody were far more interested in themselves. Investment banking for him. Nursing for her.

Married for almost sixty years. Never had kids. Most of

their long-term friends were gone. Now it was just to drink and dance and remember a full life for however long they still could.

"How you liking it out here, Wendall?"

It had taken Frank a moment to realize that was *his* name. He lifted his beer like he was about to tell them just what he thought, but Barney didn't wait.

"We been out here for around five years or so. I had sinus surgery back in '79. Can't really smell much of anything anymore, and it's nice and quiet around here. And we're both eighty-two years old. What do *we* care about brain toxins in the algae? Hell, I don't even lock my damn doors."

The rest of the conversation centered around what they were doing *now*. Mostly going back and forth from Playa Dolor to Key West. Paying a driver to take them in a rented RV.

Barney even invited them to go with them the next time. They would be heading out in a week. Frank declined, but Barney still tried to sell it.

"It ain't Fantasy Fest yet, but there's plenty to get up to."

He didn't seem bothered by Frank's continued refusal, and soon the steaks were done. In spite of her vegan brownies, Melody nodded enthusiastically when Stan offered to throw more on the grill, and when they were done according to the Bluetooth thermometers, she had complimented Stan on his perfectly cooked steaks.

Frank had to agree. The potato salad was from Aldi's, and decent. Plenty more beer inside. All in all, his most pleasant evening in nearly a month.

Barney and Melody had told them goodnight the second the last two beers in their cooler were empty. Stood to lean on each other as they took an unsteady line back down the walk.

Frank followed at a distance. Made sure they didn't fall into the marsh. Took note of which house was theirs.

They had been around a bit in the following days. Back for more beer the next Saturday. Brought a bucket of shrimp and a tray of gluten-free chocolate-chip cookies.

Then they went to Key West for a month, and Frank's distractions abandoned him.

He couldn't think about Jenny or Rory. His wife was becoming a distant memory. He saw Malick Briar's face in his dreams much more than Sarah's.

A midday walk had brought him to Barney and Melody's bungalow. His binoculars banging against his chest on their thin leather strap.

Barney had stopped the mail for their trip, but still he looked in the box. Smiled to himself when he found a flyer for Seaweed Stan's Pizza. A cartoon Italian that looked suspiciously like one of the Mario Bros sitting in a swamp boat. WE DELIVER ANYWHERE!

He took the flyer up to Barney's back door, and true to the old man's word, it wasn't locked.

He dropped the flyer on the counter, then walked through a stranger's home. One that reflected a much different life than they had spoken about. And very different from what they posted.

Much like Frank and Stan — or Wendall and Trevor — their posts were pictures of the sun and the water and food and drink. Comments on similar posts, and Melody always signing off with, *May God keep you well.*

But the interior of their home reflected a life more meaningfully lived. A timeline of photos from now to ancient black-and-whites. Professional images of suits and ties and dresses and uniforms.

No tropical decor. No Key West or Parrothead nonsense. An old console record player with a Christy Minstrels album sitting next to the Smothers Brothers doing Aesop's Fables.

Frank sat on their bed. Facing the rear window with the view of the ocean. Took in the smell of clean sheets and pain relief cream. Raised Sarah's face in his mind. Imagined her behind him getting ready for bed. Lying down. After Jenny had grown up, and they were alone again. As easy with each other as Barney and Melody were.

For the first time since standing in the rain behind the Wild One gym, Frank put his head in his hands and cried.

Chapter Four

FRANK WENT BACK the next day.

Stan had gone into town. Squeezing into the driver's seat of the Chevy Spark they were using instead of Frank's Avalanche or one of Stan's many trucks.

Frank refused to drive the thing. He had been sitting on plenty of money since Sarah's suicide, but had treated himself to only a single luxury. His red Avalanche, now sitting in a Wildwood barn. Along with everything that identified him. Including notes and plans. Maybe a dream or two.

Mo and Gen were living off the grid in a house they had bid on years ago. A quiet spot where they could build a future. And treat veterans with brain trauma.

Frank's obsession had ended those dreams as well, and it was another thing for him to try to bar from his mind. He never wanted their help in the first place, but Stan had worn him down. Told him how much he *needed* their help.

Frank wanted to blame Stan, but he couldn't. He could barely blame himself. It wasn't his fault, but it was *because* of him.

He sighed with a stretch. Lay back to look up at Barney's bedroom ceiling. Crossed his hands over his belly. Imagined what it would be like to have Sarah moving around in the house with him. Just *somebody* sharing space.

He was tired of feeling lonely. Like nothing was *his* anymore.

Even his choices didn't belong to him. Until they could get a little clear air, he couldn't even look into the building in Tallahassee. He had to wait, wait, wait.

When he sighed in frustration, his binoculars slid off his chest to fall into the gap at his side.

He lifted his head off the bed to look down at them.

Sat up with a grunt of habit rather than effort. All those crunches GG had made him do paying off in such a small way.

He slid to the edge of the bed. Leaned forward to look out the bedroom window.

Barney lived right around the curve of the beach. Frank could see the bungalow through the trees from his front porch, but all the other houses in Playa Dolor were hidden. Barney's window faced the ocean at an angle to get a good view of the beach as it curled away into the distant trees.

Cabins and cabanas that Frank couldn't see from his end of the beach were visible from Barney's bedroom window. One nestled back in the marsh. The same stilts his cabin sat on turning green with the creeping algae. Farther down was a cottage right up to the sand. Another peeking out from the adjacent trees. Another so far away it was reduced to a speck in his vision.

He pulled up the binoculars. Steadied them against the glass. Focused on the far house.

It was just a beach house. Nothing fancy or special.

Gray and white. Curtains thrown back. Movement on the screened porch.

A trail through the sand led to a pier extending into the surf, a boat bobbing at the end of a rope.

He brought his focus up along the beach to the next house. Much like that distant cabin, it was a generic home that said *beach* with every angle and color. A small trailer with a pair of jet skis strapped to it. A flashy grill sitting out in the open. No screened porch or patio roof or *anything* that might protect from the sun.

There was no pier for this house, but Frank could make out the shape of a matching shed in the trees behind it. The next house was sitting like it had grown from the marsh. Algae covered the vinyl siding like it was being reclaimed by nature. Frank thought about the dream he kept having about Malick Briar. The shining skull poking out of the slimy growth in the stinking swamp behind where Stan's gym had been.

He closed his eyes with a shudder. Pulled the binoculars down while drawing a steadying breath. He raised them again, now aimed at the beach. To the nearest pier that went with the algae-soaked house he had just been looking at.

He went to the end of the railing jutting out over the water. Unlike the house, the pier was clean. A bright coat of white paint. Ropes and life preservers, but no watercraft.

He tracked along the pier toward the sand, and stopped with a surprised grunt when he passed over something in a blur of color. Backtracked in slow-motion.

Found what had caught his eye. Held his breath as he stared.

A woman sat on a tall stool. One hand planted

between her legs to lean forward. Studying a sheet of paper clipped to an easel.

Jean shorts cut so high, the ends of the pocket stuck out past the frayed end. A sleeveless shirt trimmed short enough to show off her ribs. Her skin was so pale, it made him hiss in sympathy for being in the direct sun. But there was a sheen to her. Sweat or sunscreen. She almost sparkled.

But it was her hair that held his attention. Curly and red. Bouncing as she moved. Fluttering in the breeze. From so far away, it looked like cotton candy. Or like a burning match head.

She held her hand against the paper. Leaned out to look past the edge.

Frank's gaze drifted down to the way the shirt settled on her breasts. Down past the flat of her stomach where her hips swelled. The flesh of her thighs straining against the tight shorts. Small ankles. The soles of her bare feet were nearly black.

The binoculars were zoomed so far in that she danced in his field of view. He pressed the eyepieces in deep. Steadied on the window. Watched her scrape color across the paper. She leaned back. Pushed hair from her face. Shot both hands into the air for a stretch that lifted the shirt to reveal the side of her left breast sagging from under the bottom of her shirt.

The low tingle of an erection caught Frank by surprise. He pulled the binoculars down with a nervous laugh. Shook his head in disbelief.

Even when having an affair — when Sarah had stopped speaking to him — Frank remembered fretting about his performance. One of those things men were never supposed to talk about.

Stigmatizing. Something for others to use as fuel for the ridicule. Or an argument late at night when logic and reason fled in the face of anger, and the need to *harm*. When the affair had ended — Frank made himself admit the truth — when he had finally been *caught*, he'd exhaled with relief. Not just because he didn't have to lie anymore, but he didn't have to deal with the anxiety of disappointing a younger lover. Even younger than Sarah …

Foolish, vain old man.

Losing his paunch and improving his cardiovascular health was doing more than the little blue pill *ever* did. Fighting to get hard, then taking the damn thing to *stay* hard — or to a marginally satisfactory degree. But a spontaneous erection was something Frank hadn't felt in quite some time.

He looked over his shoulder, as if he expected to find somebody watching him. Judging him.

He pulled the binoculars back up. Steadied them as he focused back on the pier. Scanned the entire length, but the woman was gone. Frank tracked the path up the beach and found her a few yards from the end of the boardwalk leading to the cottage.

She walked to the door, then looked back at the ocean. Like she was getting one last glance before going back inside and losing it forever.

She shielded her eyes and leaned on the doorframe.

Or like she was waiting for somebody coming home by sea.

Was she excited for his arrival? Worried?

The woman's hand fell from her forehead like it suddenly gained weight.

Then she went inside, leaving the door open behind her. He waited, but she never reappeared.

Frank whipped the binoculars out to the water, but saw nothing. No boats. No one coming home. Just the sun sparkling off the ocean. The seaweed beckoning him into the waves.

Chapter Five

THEY TOOK their beers to the beach that evening. All the way to the water where the aroma was a footnote to the heat.

The sunset was blazing toward the horizon. The sky looked like an open box of pastels.

Frank looked at Stan over the top of his bottle. Wondered why this wasn't his cousin's first choice. To live out here so close to the water in layers of privacy.

But he knew the answer.

Stan had moved to Willet County because it was right next to Creek County. So, right next to Frank.

"What?" Stan said.

Frank shook his head. "Just thinking."

"About what, bitch?"

Frank smiled. Drained his beer. Reached for another one before answering. "Why you never got married."

Stan replaced the empty bottle with a fresh one from the cooler at his feet. "We've talked about this. I just don't think I'm compatible."

Frank pulled his bottle opener out of his pocket.

Thought briefly about hanging it on a chain around his neck like Barney. "Compatible with what? An emotionally stable female? Somebody who would forgive you no matter what?"

"No, just people."

Frank sighed. "Yeah, people are difficult. But women are … tough."

Stan raised his binoculars. Small field glasses. Surveyed the beach in the distance. "Tell me about it. But why would I look for someone when I have *you*?"

"Like I'm some kind of catch?"

Stan grinned over his shoulder. "Well, you married *me*, so at least you got taste."

It felt good to joke. To talk without the weight of Malick Briar pressing them down. That colorful thought made him think of the young girls crushed under Briar's literal weight, and he closed his eyes. "I'm sorry, Stan."

He sighed. "For the thousandth time, what the fuck for?"

Instead of counting off all the ways Frank felt like he had ruined the younger man's life, he cleared his throat. "You talk to anybody?"

Stan pulled the glasses down for a swig from his bottle. He nodded. "Ian should be able to come out in a few days. Get us hooked up through a private ISP. New phones. And a bunch of info. Maybe even some insight."

"Like?"

Stan shrugged. "Like how there's hardly any word about us."

"That doesn't make any sense."

Stan looked back through the glasses. "It does if you don't want anybody else to find what you're looking for."

"You know as well as I do — if they pick us up without killing us, we won't survive the trip."

"Exactly. Why even bother with the paperwork if you can just go sport fishing south of Tallahassee with a couple buddies. Make it a long weekend. Shit, maybe even request it through your supervisor. Find a zealous yet retired detective and his much younger and more handsome cousin. Put the screws to 'em before slicing their throats and dumping them at sea."

Frank put the other beer down with a few long swallows. "Well, when you put it that way …"

Stan snorted laughter. Recovered with a shake of his head. "I'd fucking follow you anywhere, you know that?"

Frank looked down at his toes digging into the sand. "Yeah, but I don't understand why."

"I know. That's why you're so fucking adorable."

"I'm not kidding."

Stan lowered the glasses to his side. "I know, Frank. And the fact that you don't understand why you are worth following, is the reason I always will."

Frank growled in frustration. "That's pretty cryptic."

Stan grinned. "That's what attracted me to you in the first place. You like your men mysterious."

He handed the glasses over. Pointed down the beach with his beer. "Take a look at the hottie splashing in the waves down there."

Frank squinted into the distance. Took the glasses and held them up, hoping Stan meant the redhead.

He scanned up along the shore until he found her.

Stared with his mouth hanging open for longer than he had intended. Just the shape of her as she splashed and kicked the water. One half a silhouette of setting sunlight. The other half in dark relief to the background.

"That makes sense," Stan said.

Frank lowered the glasses. "What does?"

"You took an extra shower today. Shaved that dome

until it *squeaked*. Combed your beard until it was like silk, you old silver fox. Like you were going out on a date."

"Don't be foolish. I just wanted to look nice."

"For me?" Stan put his hands over his heart. "You shouldn't have."

Frank sighed and passed the glasses back.

Stan didn't take them, digging for another beer instead. "I saw her walking down the lane when I went to the library the other day. She's a medium squeezing into a small for sure, but when I turned the corner and looked back to wave …" He shook the beer in front of his face. "She has some unfortunate issues up top there."

Frank bit back a retort. Ready to defend a total stranger. Drew a calming breath. "And you think I put balm on my beard for *her*?"

"Wait a fucking minute. You actually put *balm* on your beard? Are you in love or something? Been meeting her in secret while breaking into the Hollander place?"

Frank winced. Of course Stan knew about that. He shrugged. "I just … she looks so sad."

Stan chuckled. Slapped Frank on the shoulder. "I get it, buddy. And I don't think age is that big a deal — I mean, look at *us* — but maybe you should be careful with that one. She's *damaged*. And maybe you don't realize it, but you are too."

Frank looked back through the glasses. "Sarah was younger than me."

"Right, and you were worried about it *then*."

"How can you tell she's damaged?" Frank kept looking, but now he couldn't find her.

"She's got that sort of trailer feel to her. The kind of chick that tells the cops she still loves her man even after he pastes her one."

"I saw her sitting at an easel. Some kind of artist."

Stan threw his hands up. "Hey, I ain't saying not to go for it. I'm saying be careful. Don't just jump without looking down."

Frank finally found her. Standing a few yards up from the edge of the water. Facing him with her hands on her forehead, shielding her eyes from the remaining sun. Looking right at where he stood.

He dropped the glasses and turned to Stan. There was no way she could make out any details. "I don't jump into things."

Stan tipped up his fresh beer. Worked half of it down before responding. "No, you fucking mope about it for weeks, and *still* fuck it up."

Frank burst out laughing. Nerves and shame. Like giggling at the pain of hitting your elbow on the door jamb.

He laughed harder.

Especially when you're in a hurry because there is *pressing* business.

He bent over with laughter. Caught his breath and stood to drain his beer. It burned his throat.

He blinked back the tears. "I miss them."

"I know, buddy."

"I'm tired of looking behind me and seeing her not there. I'm tired of reaching for her and feeling *nothing*."

"I'm so sorry, Frank."

"I'm tired of *needing* them, you know? If I could just not *want* to love them anymore, life would be so much easier."

He wiped his eyes before pulling the glasses back up, but the woman was gone.

Chapter Six

"WE GOT A REPORT FROM MO," Stan said. "Well, not a report ... more like a heads up."

Frank looked up from his pancakes browning on the griddle. "How are they doing?"

Stan liked his pancakes thick and fluffy. A deep layer of syrup on the plate. The pancakes on top, slathered with peanut butter. Then another drizzle of syrup. Sausage or bacon, and a fried egg — even as a grown man, he called them *drippy* eggs.

Stan made a seesaw with his right hand. "They're okay, I guess. Mo's down about thirty pounds. Sweating it out in the heat. Bitches about all the mowing. Gen is still a house. Probably working that man under the table. And GG is ... he's GG."

Frank didn't think any of that sounded *okay*. It sounded like filler. Like something to say to avoid the *real* conversation. "I miss that kid."

He flipped the pancakes.

Stan grinned. "Kid? He's well over forty. I mean sure, he wears that narwhal T-shirt all the time —"

"Or the one with the … what is it, a poop emoji?"

"Yeah, so I can see how you might see him as a kid."

Frank shrugged. "I'm seeing myself more and more as an old man. If we actually had a lawn instead of that flatulent swamp out there, I'd be yelling at kids to stay the hell off it."

He laid bacon strips in his saucer. Piling them until none of the porcelain could be seen. Slid it aside to stack the pancakes on Stan's pond of syrup. Cut the heat to the griddle before flopping the egg on top.

Frank was keeping his carbs low until the evening. Saving them up for the nightly beers. A strategy that was keeping his waistline trim, but would horrify the doctor he no longer had.

He sat with his bacon. Poured a fresh cup of black coffee. "None of that sounded like a heads up."

Stan paused in smearing peanut butter on his obscene breakfast. "Hey, Ian should be out here sometime today. Guy's got a Dish Network van. Gonna be running us a dish for the new VPN. He said the latency is gonna be so high, the Apollo crew would've been dead before they could have ever reported their problem to Houston — which is a funny joke for *him*, I guess — but it'll let us access Mo's server."

Frank nodded. Took his time on the next slice of bacon. He liked it rare. Some people called it *floppy*, but that made it sound childish. Bacon was too serious a subject for such a trivial word.

He took his time wiping grease from the corners of his mustache. "What was the heads up, please?"

Stan cut into the soggy stack before answering. "Ty Kirby." Stuffed a dripping bite into his mouth.

"The heads up was Ty Kirby?"

"Morlikesfugginshow."

More like his fucking show.

Frank remembered the last time he had watched *In Our Midst*. The pictures of Rory Day. Bound and gagged at her crime scene. His daughter … the same. Sarah played like a tragedy. Him like the cause.

Painted as the villain.

"What now?" he sighed.

Stan stabbed another huge mouthful. "It's interesting, to say the least."

Frank put his hands flat on the table. "Will you just tell me, please? Or should I watch it for myself?"

"Don't watch it while you're taking a shit. It'll make you constipated. Stick with porn."

Frank closed his eyes. Listened to his cousin chew through three more bites before rejoining the conversation.

He didn't understand a lot of men's fascination with porn. He understood its allure, just not its hold. He'd been respectful to women his whole life. Protective and gentle. Many alpha types said the only *real* way to get a woman's love and respect was to treat them the way they secretly wanted to be treated. The implication being that women wanted to be dominated.

Frank's every relationship had been the exact opposite. They had been easy and drama-free, largely because he had treated women the way he *knew* they wanted to be treated. With care and consideration.

The way he himself wanted to be treated.

People wanted to feel like they were being listened to. Like they mattered.

Porn made the women not matter. But maybe that was just one old man's opinion.

"Can it be any worse than the last one?" Frank asked.

Stan looked away. "Maybe not for you."

Frank finished his coffee. Stood and went to the pot for a refill. "What is it?"

Stan sighed. "He took a camera crew to the Tallahassee building. Like Geraldo looking for Al Capone's tomb or whatever. Found some pretty damning evidence of an underage prostitution ring doing big business right under the noses of the local authorities. Claims the thing has international ties. Federal involvement. Funds for a state task force."

Frank turned with his full cup held to his lips to blow the steam away. "A task force, huh?"

Stan nodded. "To look for the man behind the whole operation."

"Wouldn't be El Chapo by any chance, would it?"

"I'm afraid not, buddy. The picture they keep plastering across the screen is yours. With that dumb-fuck smile you whip out in public."

Frank nodded. "The blue tie?"

"That's the one."

A poorly lit headshot he had done years ago for a Creek County newsletter that made the rounds for local residents for a couple weeks. It got a poor response. A lot of letters about how taxes could be put to better use than a newsletter with grammatical errors.

The newsletter died a quick death, but Frank had found his picture stuck to everything from urinals to milk cartons. A favorite inside joke with the other officers for a while too long.

Frank took a loud sip. "So, I'm running the underage Florida sex trade. No drugs?"

"Nope." Stan shook his head. "Just the icky sex stuff."

"What about the papers? *Other* news sources?"

"As far as I can tell, it's just Kirby in the local markets. CNN had a quick clip, but it probably made a bunch of people sick enough for a recall since Kirby's sleazy smile was on ample display."

"Anything else?"

Stan nodded reluctantly. "I don't come off very good, that's for sure."

"Like a right-hand-man kind of a thing?"

"Heinrich to your Adolph, yeah."

"What picture did they use for *you*?"

Stan met his gaze. Held it through a fresh bite of pancakes.

Frank nodded as he looked away. "I understand. I just don't understand why."

"Why frame us?" Stan asked.

"No, I get that. I just don't understand Owens. And West. So keen on taking that building down. Exposing those people. Saving those girls. Only to be the ones … well, not part of the sex ring in Tallahassee, but …"

"Something worse?"

Frank thought of how Rory Day had been raped and murdered. Thought about those terrified girls being escorted into the back of the building in Tallahassee. "Not worse, really. It doesn't matter what hand those girls suffered under. It just seems darker somehow."

"More sinister," Stan whispered.

"Were they competitors?"

Stan scraped drying syrup onto the edge of his fork. "Like reducing the victim pool or something?"

Frank shook his head. Shrugged in frustration. He had been puzzling through it ever since watching his house burn down in the rearview mirror.

"The only things that make sense are the murders."

Stan tipped his head back with a sigh. "How fucked up is life when the worst thing is the one that's easiest to understand?"

Frank finished his coffee. Looked at the pot and argued with himself about making more. Could he afford that much caffeine in his system while doing sprints in the blazing heat?

He started a fresh pot.

"Using Malick Briar as a carrot for us only works if they knew they were going to frame us for the Tallahassee thing later. Why else carry the evidence around in the back of the car like that?"

Stan joined him at the counter to wait for the coffee to finish dripping. Started washing the breakfast dishes. Frank reflected on what a good couple they actually *did* make.

Stan turned while the water got hot. "A lot of serial rapists and murderers like to be close to their trophies."

"Not like that. They usually hide them. Close, surely. But in the trunk of an official vehicle?"

Stan shrugged before turning back to the sink. "They were cops, though. Above-the-law types?"

"We're missing something."

"Maybe not as much as you think."

"What do you mean?"

Stan smiled sheepishly. "Not sure, but something's tickling my asshole about this."

"That's disgusting."

Stan batted his eyes. "That's why you love me. Could you pour me a cup of coffee, my sweet Wendall darling?"

Frank smiled in spite of the bitter worry that kept bubbling hotter and hotter in his gut. "It would be my pleasure, Trevor dear."

Frank filled two cups. Slid Stan's over for him to add the cream and sugar himself. Took his own to the window to look at the rising sun trying to burn through the gathering rain clouds.

His best relationship had ended the worst. When he

stopped listening to Sarah … and when he felt like she wasn't listening to *him*. A simple thing he had been unable to provide. Blinded by selfishness.

He burned his lips on the fresh coffee. Continued drinking in spite of the pain.

Once Ian installed the new internet, he and Stan could stop treading water. They could actually dive deep again. Down to where the predators hunted — where the sunlight barely reached.

Where death was a near-certainty.

The last thing Frank had was his life, and it was worth less every day. He smiled when the next drink still burned.

Chapter Seven

BACK IN BARNEY and Melody's house. In the dark with the curtains drawn. Frank sat on the edge of their bed with the phone in his hand. He had reached for the binoculars several times, but if the woman was out there, he would never see her.

Frank had come to the beach gasping through yet another sprint he was sure would kill him. Glancing up the length of the sand to see if he could catch a glimpse of the redhead he couldn't stop thinking of.

Shaking his own head in disgust as his behavior.

He knew it was all a distraction. What benefit did the exercise really have when he was always fantasizing about how he might die? Or his lusting after a stranger?

They were just to keep his mind off reality. His inability to continue his investigation. And finally, when Ian had installed the fake Dish Network system that would get them on a private and protected internet, it was his *unwillingness* to continue that he was trying not to face.

Stan had sat down to start building back out his network of contacts, but Frank ignored it. Took a long shower. Shaved his head. Trimmed his mustache. Took a little extra care in his appearance. More than he ever used to back when he wore a tie every day.

It was odd to end up waiting so long in life to finally like the way he looked. To be *genuinely* pleased with his appearance. It was always enough that he looked *appropriate*. He never thought he had the face or body to be attractive, and it never bothered him.

He never felt handsome, despite what Sarah had often said. He felt *good*. Nice. Respectful and polite.

But losing the weight — something he had never been occupied with — suited him. As did the new hairstyle. He rubbed his bald head. Down the length of his long beard. Chuckled to himself.

He just had to wait a while for hair to fall out in one place, while it grew in another.

Like a criminal dying his hair after going on the run only to realize he looks better as a blond.

Stan raised an eyebrow when Frank came out of the bathroom. Primped and preened and dressed in dark colors. Neither one of them commented, but it still hung between them. But like Stan's obsession with food, there was a deep reason behind Frank's new fascination with the comb. Something to get teased out by a therapist.

No time for that, though. Just push it down where it will start another tumor.

Frank was worried about becoming too comfortable in Barney's house. Using it as a way to escape Stan's scrutiny. He couldn't rely too heavily on it — what would he do when Barney and Melody came back from vacation?

Another worry to push down. He looked at his phone instead of thinking any more about the complications his behavior was causing. Unlocked it with his thumbprint. Scrolled to his downloads.

He didn't want to watch Kirby's smug internet show with Stan in the other room. He needed to experience it alone, and whatever accompanied the experience.

He had downloaded the flagged video stream as a generic mpeg file — pleased with himself for navigating that technology all on his own. Saved it on his phone to watch while walking through the surf, but found himself going out the back door and walking down the gravel lane to his neighbor's place.

Dark under the hanging limbs of the willows surrounding the marsh. Humidity making the vegetal rot cling to his clothes, overpowering the sandalwood in his beard oil.

Frank went inside as though invited, reasonably sure he hadn't been seen.

He navigated through the black interior from memory. Back to sit on the bed by the window to look out at the ocean and the stars and the moon. Pulling the curtains to hide the glow of the phone reflecting off his face.

He turned the phone sideways and started the video.

The same dramatic swell of music, only this time the swooping graphics were interrupted by action shots of Ty Kirby chasing somebody with his head down. The outstretched mic bouncing with their frantic steps.

"Today, we look deeper into the Florida sex-trafficking epidemic."

His voice was different too. Deeper, with a gravel intensity. As if announcing a blockbuster.

Another action shot of him running down a sidewalk, the scene jittering all over as the cameraman tried to keep up.

"A criminal ring deeper than the roots of the community it has shattered."

Frank snorted laughter at that one.

Kirby's face filled the screen. His caring smile changed to a resolute line as the intensity in his eyes settled into a challenging stare.

His hairline was suspiciously fuller than Frank remembered. Almost straight across and thick like a forest. Artificially dark. Frank couldn't help but laugh when he realized Ty Kirby looked like Ronald Reagan.

"And the men suspected of running the entire operation? Evil that exists in our cities. In our neighborhoods. In our *midst.*"

A recap of Kirby's "findings" up to this point began, and at the sight of Jenny's picture again, Frank looked away. Thumbed the volume down to a whisper that kept him from hearing the words.

The picture of him again. Then the one looking like Frank was holding Jenny and Sarah against their will. A good wife and daughter keeping nice in public because they knew what was good for them.

The implication clear.

Then a picture of the building in Tallahassee. It cut to a man-on-the-street shot of an older gentleman pointing to the front doors behind him. Shaking his head in disappointment at the obvious decline of society.

Then shots from the interior that made the place look like a swinger's pad. An orgy of evidence showing all the orgies inside.

Kirby shaking his head in solemn appreciation of what the viewer was surely going through. Then a shot of Stan. Helmet and body armor. Sand in the background. His smile triumphant. In Afghanistan with a lumberjack's beard. Smashed under the chin strap of his Kevlar.

The image faded to black and Frank knew what was coming. A parade of dead children. Showing them chained to the wall and left for dead when the terrorists Stan and his CIA team had been tracking escaped, after the rules of engagement had taken one of many wrong turns during the conflict.

Starved to death while they waited for rescue. The reason Stan stuffed himself to near vomiting at every meal. Then punished himself with hours of grueling exercise.

But the video — even without the sound — painted Stan as a beast that had preyed on children during the vulnerability of war. Now back in the states, bringing his evil here to turn America's children into his next spate of victims.

Frank stared at the screen without really seeing it until the end where Kirby put out his plea for his subscribers to be on the lookout for evil in our midst. Where pictures of Frank and Stan faded in under a phone number. The hotline for a concerned citizen to do the right thing.

Frank closed the video before it could play out. Let the phone drop from his fingers. Threw the curtains open and leaned forward to look at the dark churning water in the distance.

The peaks of a million ripples sparkled. Danced in a hypnotizing silence.

Dark shapes formed a distance out from the beach. Frank blinked, but the shapes remained. Like negative space floating toward the pier. He lifted the binoculars. Found where the black colored out the reflections.

Boats. Two small watercraft making their way to the small dock at the end of the pier. The one that was maintained with fresh paint and straight boards. That led to the path up to the cottage where the woman had gone with her easel.

Frank wondered again what that picture had looked like.

He held his attention on the boats. Could just make out

figures climbing the stairs. Four of them. The front two were opposites. One tall. One short. Holding something between them. The two bringing up the rear were even in height and size.

Up to the small cottage. Then back to the boats for another load.

After the second trip, the figures that had been in back left the house and each got into one of the boats. They looked like small rubber dinghies. The kind a special ops soldier might use to land onshore at night.

He would have to ask Stan.

But what were they doing? Frank was sure the smaller figure in the front had been the red-haired woman. With her husband or boyfriend? He was surprised by the burning disappointment that the question stirred within him.

Maybe just a friend, then? Or an associate? But associated with what? Girl Scouts didn't deliver cookies in the dead of night.

Frank lowered the binoculars. Pulled the curtains and sat back. Maybe he would wait to tell Stan. No reason to bother him with another mystery. They had too much on their plates as it was.

He thought of Stan's prodigious meals, and laughed at his own joke as he stood and smoothed out the bed.

Chapter Eight

ANOTHER MORNING STORM brought stifling heat and humidity to the beach. Frank took a half-gallon of cold water with him, and by the time he was less than halfway done, there was only a swallow left.

He had worked his way down the beach with each set, ending up between Barney's house and the redhead's cottage. She was out on the patio with her easel, and Frank was hoping to find a reason to draw her attention.

A friendly wave. Perhaps a comment about the heat. Just her looking up and noticing him.

He bent over to put his hands on his knees. Told himself how foolish he was being while catching his breath. The air felt too thick for the oxygen he needed.

He stood and tipped back the rest of his water. Let a few drops trickle across his brow.

When he glanced at where the redhead was, he saw a man standing over her. About the size and shape of the dark figure helping her carry something from the boat. The man's hair was red as well. Much darker. Cut into a severe high-and-tight military style.

He bent over the woman. Grabbed her upper arm and jerked her to her feet. Frank straightened to turn and face them.

They seemed to notice him at once. The man pulled the woman with him as he stepped toward the door. She fumbled with her art supplies, but it was clear she would have to leave them or the man would end up dragging her behind him.

Her gaze met Frank's, then she looked away. Covered her face with her free hand. The man guided her inside. Turned to stare before stepping backward through the doorway.

He grinned and waved. *Howdy neighbor*!

Frank could hear the man slam the door all the way across the sand.

He gave an exaggerated shrug. Turned and started a slow jog back to his end of the beach. Into the wind carrying the drying stench of the marsh after the rain had churned it up.

A Partridge Pharmaceutical canoe puttered through the dark water next to the boardwalk leading back to his cabin. He waved, and the red-faced kid at the small tiller waved back.

The research interns were always out after a good rain. Especially after consecutive storms. He'd have to be careful when going out tonight. *If* he went out. He shook his head as he opened the door.

Of course he would.

The air conditioner burned across his exposed skin, and he gasped in relieved pleasure. Now that they had equipment hooked into a network, Frank could count on temperatures similar to what they had in the old Batcave. This new place wasn't as good as the old one — more of a Batcabana — but it was something to start with.

Or *re*-start.

He needed to dig back into Owens and West. Malick Briar and Pedophile Junction. But it would be hard to think of anything other than the redhead woman and what she was doing with that man at night.

He rolled his eyes at himself. It wasn't too hard to guess what they were up to at night. He wondered about the boats, though. And the hand holding her arm so tight. Probably enough to leave a bruise.

He hated that so many women were victims. Men who wielded power to dominate body and spirit. Women stunted into rigid fear and servitude.

He forced himself to calm down. To draw several deep breaths. He was projecting his own biases on the relationship he'd just witnessed. He didn't know what happened before or after. What stresses they were under.

Still, did the woman deserve the kind of treatment he'd seen?

Frank had seen some devious minds during his time as a detective, many of them female. For years, it had surprised him. Whenever he had discovered a woman capable of cruelty and manipulation, it set him back on his heels. A kind of prejudiced behavior on his part that he hadn't recognized for a while.

The day he realized that women were often as morally capable as men to harm others was the day he became a *good* detective. It kept him from prematurely ruling out reasonable possibilities. A hard thing to admit —- that he was protecting women from assuming the guilt he would only afford to men. Another form of sexism. As hard as it was to dig out as it had been, there was still some underneath.

Some assumptions that lessened another person in his estimation, regardless how innocent were his intentions.

But no matter how much Frank tried to talk through his flawed motivations and circular logic, he couldn't dismiss what he'd seen.

The man had treated the woman poorly, and Frank refused to believe she deserved it. The shame on her face at having a witness to her abuse was enough to convince him.

"You gonna stand there sweating on the tile all day?"

Stan's question startled him out of his thoughts, but Frank didn't jump. Just turned to regard his cousin leaning through the doorway. "Do we really know the people here at Playa Dolor?"

Stan shrugged as he stepped through. "We know the *kind* of people they are."

Frank almost told him about the boats. Described what he had seen during his sprints instead. Stan was smiling before he finished.

"Look. I understand how that hits your buttons. You've been a sucker for the damsel in distress your whole life. Even Sarah said so."

"What? When did you talk to Sarah?"

Stan spread his hands. "The guy might be a piece of shit, no doubt. But that kind of guy is usually the kind to keep to himself. Just like Barney and Melody. Yes, they fucked themselves into our little cookout, but they won't give a damn about what we're doing other than to tell people about the *nice gays* living on their beach."

"Stan, when did you talk to Sarah? *Why* did you talk to Sarah? She *hated* you."

Stan tipped his head in confusion. "What are you doing right now? When do you *think* I talked to her?"

"How would I know that? Why haven't you told me about this?"

"I don't know. I just assumed *she* told you."

Frank took a step. "Why were you talking to my wife?"

Stan's face shifted. From confusion to nothing. Slack flesh that showed no emotion. "I need you to think *very* hard before doing this, Frank. Whatever's got you hot and bothered—"

"Answer me!" Frank shouted.

Stan narrowed his eyes. "She called me when you were fucking that waitress."

"She wasn't a waitress!"

Stan's face went from dead emptiness to anger in a flicker. "Don't try that bullshit on me, motherfucker! You cheated on your wife with another woman. Period! End of fucking sentence! And Sarah was so desperate to keep you, she fucking called *me*! And how ridiculous is that? And you know what she told me? *Why* she hated me so much? Because she saw in you the potential to be what she saw in me. She called to ask me why you were doing this to her. Begged me to talk to you. Steer your dumb ass back home."

Frank closed his eyes. "And what did you say?"

"Come on, Frank. You know what I said. Everybody in our family died of *one* thing. The poison of our own fucking minds. Prostate cancer, strokes, heart attacks, you fucking name it, but it all comes down to worry. And fear. And choking regret. And every terrible repressed thought and memory until nothing is left but a coward who can't do himself a favor by putting a bullet into his own goddamned teeth."

Frank opened his eyes. Barely kept himself from stepping back from Stan's intensity. Held up a shaking finger. "What did you say to her?"

Stan launched the rest of the way through the doorway. Caught a handful of Frank's t-shirt at each shoulder. Drove Frank back to crash into the wall. Pushed his face in until their noses were almost touching. "I told her *no*,

Frank. I said I couldn't do it. That you were already too far gone. I hung up on your wife's fucking *sobs* because I was terrified that if you had finally fallen victim to your own demons, then what fucking chance did I have?"

He looked at his fingers entwined in the fabric of Frank's shirt. Pulled his hands away like he couldn't believe they were responding to his will. Leaned forward until his forehead was on Frank's chest. And he whispered, "I thought you knew."

Frank put one hand on the back of Stan's head. Wondered why they were so broken. Why they both struggled with the roadblocks they put in their own way. Wondered how many more people he loved would die instead of him. Like Jenny and Sarah.

Frank wanted to save that redhead down the beach. To charge in and pull her to safety. Like rescuing Freya from her father. A dopamine hit he had never felt before. And again after shooting Malick Briar. A hit he needed again … but one he was willing to let go of. For now.

And then Stan said, "If you need to do it, I won't stop you. This shit'll still be here. *I'll* still be here. Go save the girl, Frank. Just don't forget to save yourself someday."

He pushed away. Turned without another word. Frank waited until he heard his cousin's bedroom door shut before moving.

Shook his head at his own foolishness. He didn't even know her name.

Chapter Nine

FRANK REMEMBERED a career unmarred by mistakes. Most of his life lived in pragmatic care for logic and reason.

His memories were a sedate train. Each association a stop along the way. Normal and safe. Even the excitement of the job fell into predictable slots. Everything accounted for in a tidy report filed in triplicate.

Sarah had often complained about arguing with him being impossible. Mostly because he did it with so little emotion. Approaching every difference of opinion as a problem to be solved. An equation with an unknown variable. Discover what X was, and there would be no more argument.

Then a gap appeared in the tracks. His daughter disappeared, and Frank could see the impending disaster through the train's front window. And instead of slowing down, the train went faster and faster.

At first because they couldn't find her. Then because they did.

The train flew off the tracks. For the first time in his life, Frank was out of control. A problem that didn't make sense. That defied attempts at categorization. His daughter was dead. An equation that couldn't be solved, not because a variable couldn't be identified, but because it didn't even exist.

With no suspects and nobody to blame, he turned on Sarah. When that didn't bring Jenny back, he turned on himself.

The train was a jumbled heap. Smoking wreckage.

He punished himself with alcohol. No sleep. Picking arguments with anybody that would engage.

Then he cheated on Sarah, and even though Frank knew it was over, he still tried to convince himself there was a chance. Resolution. Redemption.

But they could never heal. Never go back.

She took the pills, and he took the punishment.

Now the train was a rusted shell. Weeds growing up through the shattered windows.

What was left for him now?

Was it a mistake to kill Malick Briar? He knew it had been. Even when he had pulled the trigger. And he hated himself for loving it so much.

Frank had felt satisfaction when putting a criminal away. A rapist or murderer. In the course of serving justice, he had been fulfilled and satisfied. But killing Patrick Dahl for Freya had been intoxicating.

Like discovering a thing he hadn't even known was missing from his life. Then again when he killed Briar. Frank *was* a monster, and it had felt so good, he wanted to be the monster again.

Maybe he even needed it.

The building in Tallahassee was empty. Under the control of Florida law enforcement. A task force from the Attorney General's office. As it should be. Except there were agents and officers steering the investigation away from the real criminals. Allowing them to continue abusing children ... *where?*

Next door? Another town? Another *state?*

Would it ever end?

Frank laced his shoes. Readied himself for a jog. One that would bring him to the end of the beach and back. Allow him to mentally note as many details as he could.

Stan was digging through old correspondence. Messages they had missed while waiting for Ian and Mo to connect them.

Another twinge of guilt for pulling Gen and GG into his mess. Then *another* twinge for ignoring Freya's calls. He could only imagine what she was hearing about him. Or maybe she even believed what was in the online news stories.

But she was a girl living life for the first time. Catching up on missed experiences. She didn't have time for an old man stuck into his own problems.

As his feet pounded into the sand, Frank thought about how his life might have been different if she and Irene had stayed. Maybe he could have gone to ... he didn't know what she was into other than art. A volleyball game? A school play?

It wasn't fair, him longing to live the life he lost when Jenny died. To use Freya as her replacement. And Frank wasn't the man to replace Patrick Dahl for Irene. She would have found somebody else, and he had never entertained any romantic thoughts toward her anyway.

He just wanted to offer Freya the love he could no longer give to Jenny. Have her put her head on his shoulder the way his daughter had.

Frank rolled his eyes as he picked up the pace. *Me me me ...*

He hoped there would be a reason to stop at the

redhead's cottage. Or catch her at her easel on the pier. But she was nowhere to be seen when he neared. Frank passed by without looking directly at the house. Saw nothing in his periphery. Continued on for a better lay of the land.

The houses he remembered from that first day watching out of Barney's window. Then a cluster deep inside the thickest part of the marsh going north. Small cottages arranged like a tiny community.

A few residents sitting in the shade. Breathing in the sour aroma of the algae and rotting seaweed. He waved, and the only return he got was from a bowed old lady in a one-piece standing at her porch railing.

The sand became jagged gravel. Prickly bushes and pine trees.

Frank stopped to catch his breath. Drank half his water in a couple gulping swallows. Kicked off to return home for some internet spying. Like he did back at Heirloom Cove when he was emotionally invested in finding Jenny's killer. Instead of looking for a fix.

He watched his feet churn under him as he headed back. Cursed himself for being so dramatic.

He slowed before reaching her cottage. Glanced up to see the screen door hanging open. Shifted his gaze to the pier and find her standing a few yards out, looking down between the boards.

"Hey," she called.

He skidded to a surprised stop. Lost his grip on his slick water bottle.

"Would you mind?" she said as he bent to fumble it out of the sand.

He stood and brushed sand from the bottle. "I'm sorry, would I mind what?"

She tipped her head down to look at him over the top

of her sunglasses. "I dropped my phone, and it slipped right through. Could you get it for me so I don't have to drop all this and go all the way back?"

She was barely along the pier, and there were only a few things held against her chest. One of her arms was free.

He wondered if she had been waiting for him to pass. Dropped the phone like a Victorian lady letting her hand-kerchief flutter to the ground. *Dear me, look what I've done.*

He smiled. "Absolutely."

She smiled back. "Absolutely what? You mind, or you don't?"

He waved it off. "Don't mind at all."

He crossed to the pier. Hooked to the side and knelt past one of the posts. Spent a moment adjusting to the shade underneath.

"You see it? Just in front of you there?"

He nodded as he reached. "Got it." Stood to offer it up to her.

"Can you bring it up, please?" She walked away without waiting for an answer.

Frank looked back at the cottage. Something about the dark windows made him remember the way houses in his old neighborhood seemed to be staring. *Accusing.*

He should have set the phone up on the end of the pier and waved goodbye, but Frank found himself jogging back to the end. Hopping up the three short steps to follow her.

Watched her set up the easel like he remembered, but no stool this time. Right in the boardwalk, where she sat cross-legged in front of it. Looked up to shade her eyes over her sunglasses. Reached out with the other hand. "Thanks, neighbor."

"You're welcome, neighbor."

Her fingers slid against his as she took the phone. Then

she patted the board beside her. "Have a seat, neighbor. See what I see."

He finished the last few of his water while considering an excuse to refuse her, but nothing came to mind. He resisted the urge to look at the staring cottage as he dropped into a comfortable crouch. "I'm Wendall."

She looked over at him with pursed lips. "Hmm … you don't look like a Wendall."

"Really? Sometimes I don't *feel* like a Wendall."

She laughed. "Well, I *always* feel like a Carmen. Nice to meet you."

She extended her hand, and Frank took it, surprised at the strength in her grip. "The pleasure's mine."

She opened a small box of charcoal pencils. Selected one from the end. "You one of the gay guys down at the end?"

He nodded. "I am."

She swept the pencil across the textured paper. "You don't look gay."

"Is that right? What's a gay guy look like?"

She grinned. "I don't mean it that way. I mean, you don't look like a couple."

"So how do we look?"

She rolled her eyes. "Don't get so defensive."

Frank hadn't been the least bit defensive. Just curious. Still, he ducked his head. "So, how *do* we look?"

Carmen paused with the pencil hovering over the paper. "I don't know. Like friends? Old war buddies?"

"We've been together for a long time. What about you? How long have you and your boyfriend been together?"

"My boyfriend?" She looked up in confusion, then she gave a small nod. "Oh … *him*. Feels like forever."

"He was pretty harsh with you when I saw you the other day. Or so it seemed to me."

"Things aren't always what they seem, are they, Wendall?"

Frank stood up, and both knees popped. "No they aren't, Carmen. It was nice meeting you."

He walked away without waiting for a response. When he got to the end, he looked back, and Carmen had turned all the way around to watch him leave. Frank waved before turning up the beach, and didn't wait to see if she waved back.

When he glanced at Carmen's cottage, Frank noticed that the screen door was closed.

Chapter Ten

AFTER A LONG SHOWER, and a breakfast of peppers and eggs, Frank sat at the open window with his laptop. They were expecting rain later in the afternoon, and the temperature had dropped.

A cool breeze rushed through the house. Worth it even though the rank marsh odor came with it.

He logged into the VPN with the credentials Stan had written on a Post-it Note stuck to his bathroom mirror. A small addendum at the bottom told Frank to eat the note after logging in. He settled on tearing it to pieces and tossing it on the coffee grounds in the garbage.

He started his search with satellite imaging of Playa Dolor, and his first discovery was that wasn't the beach's real name. Instead, it remained as the numerical designation of the county. The parcel map number followed by the owners' names. Arthur and Macy Daniels.

Each house was leased by the same entity — Title Holdings, LTD. Residential status was dictated by membership dues. Frank saw the yearly number and almost choked.

Ninety-seven thousand dollars.

He wondered again where Stan got his money, then the guilt reared its head. Frank was a moocher, living off of Stan's ill-gotten fortune.

What had he really been doing in the Middle East with the CIA? Or was he working for someone else entirely? Why did Stan know so many people on the fringes of the law?

People who were now in Frank's circle.

He rubbed his smooth scalp. A once nervous gesture now a habit. He brought his attention back to the screen to avoid the tangent his mind kept trying to take. A distraction he would happily feed. Just another characteristic of his failing. Avoidance, rationalization, and projection.

Focus.

It looked like the only way to discover the identity of the residents — *members* — was if they registered with the post office. The only names associated with any address he could see were Barney and Melody. From an official perspective, nobody lived in any of the cottages. Just an empty beach owned by a rich couple that leased every house to a single company.

There was also a campground with RV hookups between the marsh and the highway. Several university and company names were registered with the county in association with temporary occupancy. Frank made note of them so he could investigate later.

Stan stepped in with the car keys dangling from his finger. Looked down at Frank's scribble pad. Smiled without comment. Twirled the keys next to his head. "I'm going to the P.O. box. Then I'll pick up some steaks. Anything else?"

Frank shrugged. "Some greens? A salad?"

Stan shook his head. "Fuck that. They got ice cream on sale, though."

"Then why'd you ask?"

"I just wanted you to feel like you had a say in this relationship."

Frank covered his heart with both hands. "That's the spice that drew me in."

Stan grinned. "Some boys like to be dominated."

Frank spread his hands. "Cookies and Cream, please."

Stan blew a kiss before spinning back into the hallway.

He heard the car door shut, but the car was so small, Frank barely heard the engine. Mostly just the tires crunching over the gravel.

He looked back at the screen. Typed in the first name on the occupancy list he had made. *Altim Pharmaceuticals.* It took him to an unfinished website. Just a mission statement.

TO MAKE DREAMS POSSIBLE. WE DESIGN HOME-OPATHIC COMPOUNDS BASED ON NOVEL MOLE-CULES FOUND IN NATURE. BREAKING GROUND IN THE FIELD OF PROBABLE MEDICINE

And a *Contact Us* link. He clicked it, and got a 404 error. *PAGE NOT FOUND.*

He crossed that one off the list. Moved to the next one. Doria Natural Medicine, LLC.

He started typing, but before the search box could offer website suggestions, Frank was distracted by a knock at the door. He looked down the hallway, but couldn't see the door. He asked himself what Stan had forgotten, then shook his head with a chuckle. Stan would yell without knocking.

Frank pulled the laptop lid down until the screen turned off. Like leaving a light burning in an unoccupied room, he couldn't let the little computer use power while he wasn't there, but closing the lid all the way shut it down completely. Stan told him there was a power setting that would do what he needed better than his partial closure, but Frank didn't bother to learn something that did essentially the same thing as what he'd been doing for years.

He turned down the hallway, and his smile froze when he saw Carmen's silhouette standing on the other side of the screen.

He swallowed his surprise. Acted as natural as he could while approaching the door.

She stepped back into the light, and he saw she was dressed like she'd been when he'd spied on her from Barney's window. Cutoff denim shorts with the pockets protruding from the end of the frayed bottom. A baby tee with a collar open enough to show a bra strap. He was relieved to see it.

Pink flip-flops, but her brightly polished toes did little to hide her filthy feet.

Her hair was stylishly wild. Probably took at least an hour to look that casual.

She held up a bottle of wine. Wagged the fingers of her other hand in a wave that looked like an aborted move to push hair from her face. "Hello, neighbor."

He opened the screen door. Squinted as he stepped out. "Hello to *you*, neighbor."

She shrugged. Dug a toe into the dirt and put her hands behind her back. "I feel like I may have offended you on the pier earlier."

He waved her comment away. "Not at all."

She brought the bottle back out. "Still, I wanted to make it up to you. Would you have a drink with an apologetic friend?"

He stepped aside and motioned her through the door. "Please. Be my guest."

Her eyebrows drew down for an instant, then her face opened into a grin that deepened the lines at the corners of her mouth. Wrinkled the skin around her eyes. In this light — directly overhead — she looked much older than he had thought when they met. He wondered how old *he* looked.

She paused inside the door to kick her flip-flops off. Sauntered down the hallway. Turned into the kitchen like she knew where it was going to be. "I hope your boyfriend doesn't mind," she said over her shoulder.

"He's actually my husband, and he won't mind. Besides, he won't be back for a bit."

She stopped at the table. Spun on her toes to swing the bottle out in front of her. "Long enough to drink *this*? I don't know much about wine, so I hope it's okay."

He took it from her and looked at the label. A Pimler chardonnay 2018. "This isn't just okay, it's *very* good."

She sneered. "Good."

He turned to dig the corkscrew out of the drawer next to the sink. "Oh?"

"It's from Preston's collection."

Frank screwed the opener into the cork. "Your …?"

"The man you saw pulling me into the house." She lifted her arm, and the pale skin turned dark near her armpit. Thick dots of angry purple. Like where dug-in fingers used to be.

He released the cork. Took a slow smell coming from the open bottle. "And he won't miss this?"

She shrugged. "Fuck 'im. He's an asshole."

Frank met the intensity of her gaze. Saw pain in the lines running down the center of her forehead. The vein pulsing under her temple. He nodded. Turned to reach up for two glasses. Poured and left the open bottle sitting.

Rotated around to put the full glass in her waiting hand. "This is probably close to a hundred dollars."

She narrowed her eyes in an impish grin. "I'm worth it."

He touched his glass to hers. "I think you might be."

She touched her fingertips to the skin at the hollow of her throat. "Why Wendall, that was certainly neighborly."

The aroma filled his nose as they drank, replacing the marsh that had filled the house with its distant rot. Then he caught *her* scent. Cocoa butter, and something darkly floral.

She lowered her glass. Closed her eyes in a soft moan of pleasure. "My, that *is* good."

Frank wondered what he was doing. Wondered why he had no answer for himself.

Her eyes were pale green. Freckles made her cheeks appear rosy. Her chin came to a slight point, divided by a soft cleft. She tipped her head, and a poof of her hair parted to the edge of a deep scar in front of her ear.

He must have reacted, because she turned away, and her smile faded. She leaned back and tipped her glass up to finish it off with two matching swallows.

Stood on her toes. Put one foot in front of the other like walking a tightrope. Walked across the kitchen while looking up at Frank from under her brows. Through the thick fall of her hair.

She held her glass to the side as she leaned in. Reached around him. Her breasts brushed across his forearm.

She pulled the bottle out. Took a step back and poured herself another glass. Looked at him with one eyebrow raised in a dare.

He finished his first glass the same as she had. Lowered it for her to fill. She met his gaze through the ripple of the glass as she let the final drops fall. This time, Carmen pressed her breasts into him as she put the bottle back on the counter.

He caught his breath, but made no other sound or move. Just waited for her to step back, where she held her glass in another toast.

The clink, then they drained their wine in unison. She licked her lips. Passed her empty glass to him. Trailed her finger up his arm as she walked back into the hall. "Now that we're neighbors, let's not be strangers."

He leaned his head out to watch her walk through the door. She didn't look back.

He stepped back into the kitchen. Finally exhaled. Wiped his forehead. Asked himself when it had gotten so hot.

He almost dropped the glasses putting them in the sink. Left the bottle on the counter. Started down the hallway when he noticed her flip-flops still inside the door.

She had left him an excuse to follow. He would be foolish not to take it.

Frank turned to shut his laptop all the way down since he would be gone longer than just a few minutes, but instead he found it closed.

Like somebody had shut it already. Maybe even after opening it to see what was on the screen.

He heard the patter of rain. A sprinkle that would become the overnight storms The Weather Channel had been predicting.

Then it swelled into a battering wave that had him scrambling to shut the windows in time. If the heat wasn't going to damage the computers in the other room, the rain coming in would for sure. Then a crack of thunder. Almost like a warning. Sarah telling him to be more careful. He remembered Carmen's scent, and knew he wasn't going to listen.

Chapter Eleven

Frank finally sat down after closing the house up. Turned on the AC in preparation for the humidity the storm would bring in its wake. He spared a thought for Carmen. Hoping she got home.

Then he looked at the empty bottle. Remembered her scorn at the mention of her ... boyfriend? Husband? *Fuck 'im.*

He lifted the lid on his laptop. Waited for the restart. A warning popped up saying the web browser hadn't shut down properly and asked if he would like to restore the pages he'd been looking at. He clicked YES.

The county website opened. Then the page with the results of his last search. Doria Natural Medicine, LLC. No pages matched his search, but seven entries down found mention of Doria Nature, LLC. He clicked on it, but it was a story about a non-profit group that worked on saving endangered species when government or corporate encroachment threatened their existence.

No mention of medicine, or finding compounds in

algae. So was it the same company getting occupancy permits for Playa Dolor?

He returned to his list. Put a question mark next to Doria.

Then Partridge Pharma. He knew that one. They seemed to be active on the murky water of the marsh around his house.

The fourth company name was a local branch of a community college science group. The fifth was a transport company that used freezer trucks to deliver bioactive material to labs for research. There was no associated website. Just a name and a Texas address. Stit AC out of Galveston.

Then Terralan Pharmaceuticals. The first legitimate website he had found. Polished and professional. Pages full of up-to-date information. A company that appeared to be collecting the neurotoxins in the algae for actual research. Leaders in finding novel compounds for medicinal use in cancer treatments.

Then a permit for Ultan Mass. A Florida P.O. box, but no website.

The last occupancy permit was for Victory Care. Another Florida P.O. box, and a website with an empty FAQ and a *Contact Us* link that opened an AOL email prompt.

Frank sat back and crossed his arms. If Carmen had actually looked at his screen while he was pouring, what would she have seen? The Doria Natural Medicine search results.

So she saw what he was researching. It didn't seem to be a legitimate company anyway. Like most of the rest.

He tore the page from his notepad. Wrote the names of the one company that seemed real, Partridge Pharma, and the science group from Jenkins University. He made a quick search and found their website. Not a community college after all, but a virtual school. Still, if their internet presence was to be trusted, they were real. The rest?

Broken websites and P.O. boxes — or nothing but a name.

Frank thought back to the times he had heard a puttering boat cutting through the duckweed and algae that wasn't a Partridge intern. Stirring up the smell. The same people with the same equipment, but he couldn't remember any markings. Or information more than what Stan had told him.

He hadn't seen any freezer trucks. No company vehicles. So then what were the companies occupying?

Frank looked at the county website again. Found the permits and saw they were all up to date. They had permission to use the facilities in the campground, but no actual presence. Except for Terralan, Partridge, and Jenkins University.

Frank opened a fresh search window. Typed in *Carmen Ulta*. No result.

Carmen Mass. An obituary from Miami dated 1997.

Carmen Stit. A listing in Denver.

Carmen Victory. A drag queen in New Orleans.

Carmen Altim. No result.

Back around to the search she may have seen when she opened the laptop. *Carmen Doria.*

Three entries down was a LiveLyfe page. No profile picture in the preview. Frank clicked it, and sat back in defeat when a pop-up told him he wasn't authorized to view that page. Would he like to log in?

He almost slammed the lid shut. Held himself to closing it halfway with as much anger as he could put in the gesture. Not enough. He could log in as Wendall, but she might see him creeping on her profile, and that was clearly impolite.

He sat up with a hiss of surprise at the sound of their back door banging open. Stan burst in with a row of plastic bags hanging from his forearms. The rain was like a radio tuned to static.

Frank sighed in sudden understanding. *Static.*

He stood as Stan rushed into the kitchen. "You could have taken two trips."

Stan grunted from the effort of lifting the bulging bags to the counter. "You kidding? It's some Noah shit out there."

"Then good job, I guess."

Stan grinned over his shoulder as he dug into the first bag. "Wait'll you see what I got."

Frank nodded. "Steak and ice cream, right?"

Stan shook his head as he started unloading an ice cream truck's worth of ingredients. The Inside Scoop would be envious.

At the thought of the ice cream shop he used to take Jenny to, Frank looked away to watch the rain running down the window. It was one of the things Ty Kirby had used against him. The interview where he had said never being able to take his daughter there again was what he regretted the most.

Patrick Dahl had used it against him too. Until Frank had jumped across the table and gave the monster a beat down. Paid for the pleasure with an arrest and an interrogation. The captain had let him go, though. Dahl hadn't pressed charges, and Frank still had some pull with the older officers. The ones that remembered his service before the accusations shot like cannon balls against him.

He sighed again.

"What's wrong, buddy? How can you be sad when I got this many sprinkles?"

Frank looked away from the window. "What's in Galveston?"

Stan shrugged. "I don't know. Monkeys and sharks. Some good fishing."

"What about freezer trucks?"

Stan pulled his hands out of the bag. Turned to lean against the counter. "Yeah, those too."

"Static."

Stan narrowed his eyes. "What?"

"No." Frank shook his head. "*Static* and *Stit AC* are the same thing, right? Not terribly clever, but pretty effective."

"How'd you find that out?"

"You forget, I'm a detective."

Stan rolled his eyes as he pushed off the counter. "No, I mean *how* did you find it out? Is this a hole I need to plug now?"

"Where did you get the money for all this?"

"All of what?"

"This house? The membership to Playa Dolor? Plot 1837BG? The Wild One gym? To pay for Ian and his *services*?"

Stan crossed his arms. "You want chocolate syrup or caramel?"

"Chocolate."

Stan nodded. "Fine."

He went back to the bags. Reached up for two bowls. Slid the drawer out to fish out the ice cream scoop. As he built two huge servings of ice cream — cookies and cream slathered with syrup, Reese's Pieces, and a pillow of whipped cream — Frank wondered what his cousin would say.

Stan handed Frank his bowl. Tossed a spoon that Frank barely managed to snatch out of the air. "Here's the thing, Frank," Stan said through a bite of ice cream. "I'm not gonna answer your question. I'll say Saddam Hussein had less golden toilets when I left Baghdad, how's that?"

"Fewer, you mean?"

"What the fuck *ever*. The point is, don't fucking ask. It's enough for me to spend in four lifetimes. Even funding your nonsense—"

"It's not nonsense!"

Stan stuck the spoon in to free his hand to point at Frank's face. "It's a figure of speech. You know I don't mean it. You're just deflecting. Shut the fuck up."

"Fine."

"You don't want to know. You just think you do. Like this girl you're suddenly in love with. Like the killing you think you want to do. The children in Tallahassee. You wanna do something? I mean, *really* do something? Then let me know. Maybe I'll tell you then. In the meantime, you haven't earned the fucking right."

Frank ate with methodical bites. Barely tasting the ice cream. He knew less than when he started. Finally, he laid his spoon on the edge of the bowl. "Are you helping me, Stan?"

"Of course I am."

"But *only* me?"

"Hell no. I'm funding shit that would make you go to confession."

"I'm not Catholic."

"Exactly."

Frank snorted laughter. It kept him from crying. "Well, at least I know her name now."

"You *are* a detective."

Frank could think of only one thing to say, and it turned the ice cream sour in his belly. "Fuck you, Stan."

He grinned and took up his spoon for another bite. "You are something special, you know it?"

Frank nodded. "You should probably change the name of your occupancy permit company."

"Nah. You only figured it out because you know me. None of these people do. Besides, the *real* owners of Stit AC are Arthur and Macy Daniels."

"Are you Arthur or Macy?"

Stan grinned around his spoon. "Hopefully the rain stops before it gets too late. I still wanna grill some steaks."

Frank didn't know if he could put protein on top of half a bottle of wine and so much sugar, but he was sure going to try.

Chapter Twelve

FRANK WADED OUT into the evening surf. Out to where his feet sank into the cold muck. Toes digging into the seaweed roots.

Until the water was up to his throat. Shallow waves lifting him off the bottom. Pushing him to shore. The trough pulling him back out to sea.

He closed his eyes. Blew all his air out. Settled under the surface.

The water dipped low enough to expose his ears to the sounds above. Then it washed past into a swell of noise. He tipped his head up for a fresh breath. Blew it out so his feet cut back through the bottom.

A gentle rhythm. Like the artificial heartbeat Stan had used when Frank was gripped by a panic attack. A gentle fist on his shoulder.

The wave swept by. A deep breath. The water swallowed him, and he exhaled.

His fingers tingled. Light burst behind his eyelids.

What drove him? What *rewarded* him?

Much like funerals, revenge was for the living. It offered no solace to the victims. Or loved ones long dead.

Sarah didn't want him to kill. Jenny certainly wouldn't have wanted it. Frank's obsession was for him. It was to make him feel better for having failed his daughter.

But did he *really* fail her?

How could he have stopped it? Frank was there for her and Sarah. As perfect a life as he could have wanted. He retired after getting shot. He had plenty more time for love.

While clocking in every day, Frank had been aware of being so much older than Sarah. Being a new father at such an advanced age. An old man even before Jenny's graduation.

But being home with them had made him feel young again. For years, he had understood what Sarah had been trying to convince him of. That their life together was priceless.

Another wave … another breath, and Frank pushed himself out until he could no longer touch the bottom.

Then a rapist had stolen that new life from him. A murderer snatched it away. And even now, that thought sounded so selfish. For what had Sarah lost? And a question he had never bothered asking. *What had Jenny lost?*

Frank could only see it in terms that affected *him*. Because he was selfish. Yes, he had lost his daughter. An evil man had stolen her. But he hadn't lost Sarah. Instead, he had driven her away. Pushed her out of the only comfort she wanted. So desperately that the denial finally killed her.

Another wave drove him under. He stroked to the surface for a breath. Water rolled over his head. Pushed him back down.

After Jenny's body had been found, Frank had only

ever acted for himself. Playing the role of an enraged father. Swearing to find the man that had hurt him so …

He opened his eyes in the cold blackness, and he suddenly understood what Stan had meant. About *deserving* it.

First he had to admit it.

He pushed against the water to reach the bottom again. He looked up as his toes dug through the churning silt. The faint light was much farther away than he expected. A hazy twinkle on the waves well above his head.

He pushed off the bottom like an arrow. Clasped hands breaking through to the air where he took in a deep breath. Floundered on the surface until he oriented himself to face the shore.

He was more than a hundred yards out. Dropping between the waves. Rising in the sweep that pushed him out even more.

He put his head down and swam back to shore. Working against a current that wanted to keep him back and hold him down.

His feet finally scraped the bottom, and he stood to fight against the waves pushing him over. A few staggering steps to bend over and catch his breath. Shoulders burning, Chest heaving.

He made it out of the water. Left his shirt and sandals sitting on top of a dune. Down the boardwalk past the solar fairy lights hanging from the railing — already losing their charge and fading like dying fireflies.

He stepped quietly into the house. Shivered in the chill air. Down the hall to Stan's room. He crept inside and looked up to find him sitting up with his pistol aimed at Frank's chest.

Stan sagged in relief. Shook his head as he slid the gun back under his pillow. "The fuck you doing in here?"

Frank sat on the edge of his bed.

Stan pulled away. "Are you *wet*?"

Frank nodded. "Yeah. I just got back from a swim."

"In *that* current? What is it …?" He squinted at the bedside clock. "It's three in the morning."

"I know what you mean. What you've always meant."

"What are you talking about?"

"It's all ever been for *me*. Never for Jenny or Sarah or Rory Day. Not even for those girls in Tallahassee. But *me*."

Stan pushed himself back to rest against the headboard. "You think that's what I meant? That your intentions should have been … what? More selfless?"

Frank shook his head. "No, I don't think that's it at all. I think you just wanted me to admit it. You don't care about my intentions. It didn't matter if you believed them or not. It was about *me* believing it. Well, I believe it, Stan. I want him dead. Not for Jenny. *For me.* I want Owens gone. Not for those girls, but for *me*. Of course I care about the victims … for the ones still waiting their turn at abuse, but God help me, I want it for *me*."

Stan leaned his head back to rest on the wall. "Why?"

Frank bit back tears. Pressed his lips against the burning in his throat. "Because after she died, I forgot what it was like to feel good. To feel *anything*. Until I shot Dahl. It made me remember what it was like to feel good. Then Briar, and then that awful nothing again. I just want to feel good."

Stan sighed. Pulled his head off the wall. "You realize therapy would have been a lot easier than this, right?"

Frank blew a chuckle out of his nose. Shook his head. "Maybe, but Dahl would still be raping his daughter. And Briar would still be raping girls in Tallahassee."

"So, what do you want?"

"I want to kill them. Every single one I find. I don't

want an investigation or a trial. I want them dead. And there's so many … my God there's so many."

Stan scrubbed at his eyes. "Well, I'm proud of this breakthrough. Or whatever you wanna call it. Yes, Frank, that's what I wanted to hear, I was just hoping confession could come at a reasonable hour."

Frank threw his hands up in mock disgust. "Is anything ever good enough for you?"

Stan laughed. "I only ever ask for progress. Just as long as you're trying."

Frank sighed. "The foundation of every good relationship."

Stan leaned forward and grabbed Frank's shoulder. "This is not a righteous man's life, buddy. It's not a simple job. I've been doing it long enough to know. But it's a *necessary* one. The system failed your daughter. It failed *you*. How many more will it fail, if men like us don't do the hard things?"

Frank nodded. "I just didn't expect …"

"It to be so easy? To be a criminal? A fucking murderer?"

Frank nodded.

Stan threw his head back and laughed. His voice echoed off the ceiling like there were two of him. "You think *this* is easy? Get the fuck outta my room. We got lots to talk about tomorrow. Lots to do."

"I don't know if I can sleep."

"Well I can, so fuck off."

Frank sat for a moment before nodding. "I got your bed wet."

"Tell that to the next person that thinks we're not really gay."

Frank barked surprised laughter. Stood with a grunt of

effort. Retraced his wet steps out of his cousin's bedroom. Stan was already snuggled back in by the time Frank closed the door.

He stood in the hallway wondering why nothing felt any different.

Chapter Thirteen

FRANK STOOD in the kitchen like he'd never seen the room before. Finally, he made a decisive nod at the coffee pot. Might as well greet the sunset with a cup of joe.

Waited for it to brew like he was standing in front of the microwave waiting for the corn to pop on movie night.

He'd take his cup to the dunes. Watch the sun hit the water as it rose over his shoulder. Gather his shirt and flip-flops. Make a big breakfast ... with a lot of carbs. His idea for once. Pancakes with syrup and whipped cream.

He poured his travel mug full. Turned to head out, but froze in the doorway when he saw Carmen's flip-flops. He scooped them up as he left. A side quest of returning her shoes. Leave 'em in front of the screened-in porch door. *Then* back to the dunes for a sunrise and coffee.

He tucked the soles in his waistband. Squeezed dampness out of his beard. Almost started whistling.

He shook his head at himself. His manic behavior was disturbing. Especially in light of Stan's therapy comment.

He shrugged it away. He was fine. He had just made a

decision. Given himself direction. It always felt good to be on track.

The right track, though?

He was completely dry by the time he got to Carmen's cottage. The sky was still black, but the stars had faded. Or they were covered by clouds left over from the earlier rain.

There were no lights on in the house. Nothing but the glow of solar lamps lining the walk up to the house, making the black shade of the marsh it was sitting in look like a bottomless pit.

Frank didn't creep. He kept a normal pace toward the house. Just a guy returning his neighbor's shoes. Nothing to see here.

He pulled Carmen's flip-flops from his waistband. Stooped to line them up in front of the door. Thought better of having something right in the way. Slid them over a bit. Nodded to himself as he stood. Drank the last swallow of coffee as he turned to walk back down to the beach.

Rustling movement from him made him freeze. Rooting himself so he could listen. Might have been his imagination.

Then he heard the movement again. From inside the screened-in porch. The soft ratchet of the door spring. He turned back, ready with a smile and his neighborly excuse, then sagged in silent relief when he saw the shape of Carmen's shaggy red hair surrounding her head like an unruly bouquet.

"Hey, neighbor," she whispered.

He waved his empty coffee mug. Kept his own voice at a whisper. "Hello, neighbor." He pointed at the flip-flops. "I brought your shoes back."

She looked down, and when she looked back up, her face was open in a wide grin. She came to him on prancing tiptoe. Grabbed his bare arms with both hands. He suddenly wished he had worn a shirt.

Hers was a mid-sleeve baseball jersey. Down to the middle of her thigh. "That was so sweet of you."

Her hair brushed across his shoulder as she released him to step down her walk. "Come with me." She lifted a finger over her shoulder. Curling it in a gesture for him to follow.

Frank looked back at the dark house. Hurried to catch up. Two sets of bare feet hardly making any noise.

When they stepped out of the dark of the overhanging trees, her pale legs seemed to glow beneath the hem of her shirt. Frank looked up to find the stars back out and twinkling. The sky's edges just starting to brighten with the coming morning.

She danced across the sand to the steps of the pier. Reached back to grab Frank's hand before jumping up to the boardwalk. He wanted to snatch it away, but let her pull him up instead. Barely held in his hissing sigh when she dropped his hand.

Then she pressed up against him like they were out for a walk on their first date. Hanging on his arm like he was escorting her to the car.

He glanced back at the dark cottage. Down to her where he saw nothing but a flutter of thick hair in his face. Sweat and cocoa butter. Wine from her breath.

"Why were you sleeping on the porch?" he asked.

She sighed as she pushed off of him. His skin was hot where she had made contact. "I wasn't sleeping."

"I'm sorry."

She shook her head. "No ... Preston and I had a fight."

He remembered the bruise on her arm. The scar in her hairline. "A fight?"

"Well, an argument. We're going out of town tomorrow, and I'll have to sit for hours in the car while he gives me the silent treatment, so why not start early?" She shrugged, spreading her hands out and smiling. "He wanted me to … it doesn't matter. He was very angry, and I didn't want to hear his bullshit anymore. So, I took a bottle of wine to the porch to listen to the rain and wait for a friend … and *you* showed up."

She stepped in front of him. Pulled him into a hug, pressing her cheek against his chest. He wondered if it had only been *one* bottle of wine.

She pulled back and looked up at him. Her hair fell away from her face, and he realized she was lovely. Like a revelation. The deep lines around her mouth. The crinkling skin next to her eyes. The scar tracing toward her cheek. Signs of a life lived.

Her grin sparkled under the brightening sky. "Then you came along. Thanks, friend."

She released him to spin away. Dancing the last few steps to the end of the pier. Frank thought she was going to dive in, but she held up at the end. Rose on her tiptoes and lifted her hands overhead. The jersey rode up to the nothing underneath.

Carmen finished her stretch. Dropped to sit on the edge and patted the boards. "Come sit with me, friend."

Frank made sure there was a foot between them when he lowered onto his seat. Set his empty mug beside him. Leaned back to anchor himself and tipped his head back. Inhaled the breeze blowing off the water. Banishing the reek of marsh behind them. "I don't know if this is such a good idea."

"What? Two friends sitting together to watch the sunrise?"

"What if … Preston was it? What if he finds you gone? Comes looking for you?"

Carmen scooted sideways. Closing the distance between them. Frank had nowhere left to go. "Don't be afraid of *him*."

Frank couldn't help laughing. "I'm not afraid, Carmen. At least, not for *me*. I would feel terribly if you suffered for something I did."

She looked over her shoulder at him in surprise. "Oh," she gasped. Then she scampered up onto her knees to turn and face him. "That's the nicest thing a man has ever said to me. *Ever*."

She gracefully lifted her right leg and swung it over him, planting herself in his lap. He heard his mug splash into the ocean. He tried to sit up, but his balance was back on his hands. Then her weight pressed against his chest, driving him down. He lifted his hands to grab her waist as she darted her head forward to cover his mouth with hers.

Her breath mingled with his. Her hair covered his face like a gentle curtain. Blocking out light and sound. Nothing but her gasps and moans. His own harsh voice.

She lifted her hips far enough to reach down to his shorts. Fumbled for a moment before pulling with a growl. The bottom tore open, and the zipper lowered like tearing cloth.

When she freed his erection, he threw his head back so hard it hit the boardwalk with a thump that sent a spark of light exploding behind his eyes.

She rose up to grab the bottom of her shirt. Pulled it up over her head. Her skin was bone white.

He reached down and she slapped his hand away, so he grabbed her breasts while she guided him inside, and he blew all his breath out. Held his throat closed as a distraction against her sliding down.

He was too old for this. Desperate to last long enough to avoid embarrassment. Then he craned his head up to look up at the sun coming over the top of the trees. Putting them in view of anybody who happened to look.

She grabbed a fistful of beard in each hand. Pulled his face up. He gritted his teeth against the pain. Went where she directed. Tasted the wine on her tongue.

Spots formed in front of his eyes from holding his breath against the inevitable.

She turned her head. Drove her mouth into his shoulder. Shuddered against him with a moan stifled against his flesh, and he finally took in air. Followed by an orgasm that made his calves cramp.

She drove her forehead against his chest. Curled like a cat and threw her hair back. Planted her hands flat on his ribs. Pushed her weight down until they both relaxed.

Frank didn't dare look behind them. Looked at her face instead. At her satisfied smile. Like she had proven somebody wrong. "You made a mess," she teased.

"I'm sorry."

What a lame, old man thing to say.

She covered her giggle, then curled forward when another shudder rippled through. Frank hissed as his muscles tightened, and the cramp in his calf came back. He wanted to reach down and dig his knuckles into it, but there was no way he was pushing her off.

She sighed as she lay on top of him. Rising with his breath. "Thank you, friend."

"It was the neighborly thing to do."

She laughed. Then threw her leg back over with a low moan. Sat back on her heels as she pulled on her shirt. Bent over to hang her face in front of his. "We could all use a neighbor like you."

She kissed his forehead. Got her feet under her and stood to pull the shirt tail over her hips. Walked away without looking back.

Frank put his softening, sticky penis back in his underwear with a grimace of distaste. Rolled over to get to his knees. Held his shorts closed as he walked down the pier. Shielded his eyes from the sun. Looked back one last time before walking up the boardwalk to his cottage.

He couldn't quite make sense of what had just happened. Wondered if he'd tell Stan. Wondered if she'd tell Preston.

Then he realized his coffee cup was gone, but he wasn't going to fish it out of the seaweed. Carmen said they were going out of town. He'd get it then … and maybe find some other things, too.

Chapter Fourteen

STAN WAS ALREADY AWAKE. Gathering ingredients in the kitchen for what would probably be another epic meal. Tom Jones coming out of the Bluetooth speaker next to the sink.

Stan turned with a wooden spoon raised to his mouth like a microphone. Face tensed to belt out a line. Then he saw Frank, and his mouth fell open. Eyebrows shot up in surprise. "Da fuck?"

Frank kept his shorts closed with one hand. Waved with the other as he crossed to his chair at the small table.

Stan shut the music off. Pointed at Frank's feet. "Where are your shoes?"

He closed his eyes in frustration. Leaned his head back. "I left 'em out on the sand. Along with my shirt. I got … busy doing something else."

Stan leaned back against the counter. "And what might that something else be?"

Frank sighed. Looked down his nose at Stan before bringing his head back straight. "You know the redhead?"

"The one with the caboose?"

Frank didn't like that term, but he also didn't want to argue. "Yes. Her name is Carmen Doria."

"Good for her. What are you trying to say, Frank?"

He sighed. "I don't think she believes I'm gay anymore."

The wooden spoon fell from Stan's slack fingers. He dropped to catch it. Juggled the thing from hand to hand before finally getting it in a double grip like he was brandishing a sword. "Are you fucking serious right now?"

Frank clenched his jaw against his grin. Nodded. "Afraid so."

Stan pointed the spoon at his chest. Like a laser was going to come out. "You and her … wait. How was it?" Then he winced and flapped his hands. "Never mind. I don't need to know. Just, what the actual fuck, bro?"

Frank told him what happened. Just a clinical recounting of the events at hand. No details. No emotions.

It disgusted Frank that he wanted to crow. That it made him feel more like a man than he had in a long time. But he knew better.

"She playing you?"

Frank nodded. "Of course she is."

"What's she want?"

Frank shrugged. Told him about her probably seeing his search on his laptop. Worked his way around to how he found out about Stit AC. By then, the steaming breakfast was in front of him, and he couldn't wait to dig in.

He could barely swallow fast enough.

Stan smirked. "It's almost like you've been expending some energy."

Frank washed down some buttered wheat toast with coffee Stan had sweetened with blue agave nectar. "I haven't slept, either. But I'll nap before I go over there."

"What do you mean, *go over there*?"

Frank took another bite. Used his fork as punctuation. "She said they were going out of town tonight. So, I'm gonna wait until they leave, then I'm breaking in."

His heart raced with excitement. His cheeks felt like they were sunburned.

"Like how you used to do with your neighbors back on Heirloom?"

"Kind of, yeah." Then he told Stan about the boats. About Carmen and Preston and two others carrying something up to the cottage.

Stan sat up with interest. "Like what kind of something?"

Frank shrugged. "It was dark. It could have been *anything*. Bigger than a breadbox."

"Drugs?"

"Maybe, but it would have been quite a lot."

"A body?"

"A small one, maybe."

"Like a child?"

"Wrapped up, or in a bag?"

Stan shrugged and sat back. "Fucking bootleg movies for all we know."

"That's why I'm going over there."

Stan stabbed a fresh bite. Melted cheese made a sagging trail all the way to his mouth. He pointed at Frank's face. Swallowed the half-chewed omelette. "Just be sure you know what you're doing. And know your *why*."

Frank felt suddenly tired. Like a lead blanket had been draped over his shoulders. The thought of finishing the meal churned his stomach. "I know why I'm doing it."

"Thank Christ *one* of us does."

Frank dropped his fork. Stood without recognizing Stan's comment. Stumbled down the hall to his bedroom. Emotion and fatigue catching up with him.

He fell face first onto his bed. Thought about a shower. Brushing his teeth. Then the darkness called, and he relaxed right into it.

When Frank next opened his eyes, he blinked away the light streaming into the window. The sun blazing in late afternoon glory. He groaned and turned his head away. Winced as the ache in his neck spiked pain into the center of his head.

Pushed up off the bed. Rubbed his hands across his scalp. Hissed in pain when his fingers found the small lump in back.

He held his hand toward the bathroom. Looked through squinted eyes. Tripped over his shorts when they fell to his ankles. He hopped to catch his balance. Slammed into the door jamb. He felt hungover.

He had done *some* drinking. Lots of exertion in the heat. Then in the water. Then on the pier.

No sleep.

He found his way under the spray of a cold shower. Made himself stand there until he was completely awake. Heart pounding. Deep breaths and shivers.

Frank felt more normal by the time he finished drying off. Just aching joints, a throbbing head, and red skin. Eyes that felt like they were full of sand. He wiped off the mirror. Looked at the dark bags under his eyes. Of *course* he was being played.

He got dressed in fresh shorts. A T-shirt that would have been too small six months ago. Sneered at his own vanity as he brushed his beard out until it was shiny and dry.

Stuffed the buttonless shorts and crusty underwear he had been wearing into the trash. Walked out barefoot to the kitchen, but Stan wasn't there. He glanced down the hall. Walked to the door, and the car was gone.

What more was there to talk about anyway?

Frank threw open the door and stomped down the boardwalk. Cursing himself for a fool. Cursing his dumb penis. His dumber brain.

He wanted to go for a run. Or another swim. He thought of Carmen in her baseball jersey nightshirt. Thought of something else he could go for. Then he shook his head. That's what she wanted. To distract him. But from what?

Or was it possible that she wanted just what she got? A little friendship. A quickie to get back at her man. Physical pleasure while in a joyless relationship with an abuser … but with an old man like him?

He was at least fifteen years older than her. Thanks to the gym, he had the body of a much younger man — probably better than the body he'd had in college — but he still had the face of a man used hard by life. The Santa beard. Spider veins along his shins.

This isn't what he should have been thinking about.

He got to the dune where he had dropped his shirt and shoes yesterday. Sighed in frustration when he found them embedded in a layer of slimy sand. The tide pulling marsh water across the beach.

He shook his head as he turned to head toward the Doria pier. Maybe he could find that coffee cup. Then he slowed. Thought about waiting until they left. Then gave himself a mental slap.

No big deal if Carmen saw him. He'd smile and wave and take his cup home. If *Preston* saw him … he'd do the same thing. Give Frank a chance to see the man's face.

He angled into the surf. Walked the distance with the waves splashing up to his knees. A few feet from the pier, and he saw it. The tide well out from where it had been earlier.

His cup flashed from a small mound of sand next to a pole stained black with creosote. He went right for it. Pulled it out to let the gunk at the bottom fall out in fat plops at his feet.

The sound of the screen door slamming made him look up with a jerk. The sun was behind him. Shining onto the cabin's face. Showing Preston in clear relief as he walked down his boardwalk toward the beach.

Frank plastered on a smile. Waved as he splashed back up to the dry sand. Preston didn't wave back.

His hair was dark brown this time. Recently colored. Orange and red highlights along its length. Plastered to his head with some product that made it look like strands of yarn lying in perfect lines from a sharp part on the side.

A banana boat tan. Board shorts under a white tank top that showed off his burned shoulders. He was taller than Carmen, but probably weighed less.

His smile reminded Frank of Patrick Dahl. Like the man knew a secret he couldn't wait to share. Before he could open his mouth in greeting, Preston said, "You one of the fags from down on the end?"

Frank couldn't help feeling offended. It didn't matter if it was true or not, it was aimed at him, and he didn't understand why the man wanted to be so rude upon their introduction. He took a deep breath. "Isn't that a tad insensitive?"

Preston nodded, and his smile became a grin. "Probably. What are you doing snooping around my pier?"

Frank stood up straight. Even with all the weight he had lost, he was bigger than this man. But he still needed to be careful. "Which question do you want answered first?"

His grin faded into confusion. "What?"

"Well, as to the first — yes. I am one of the fags. As to

the second — I wasn't snooping. I was simply looking for something of mine I had lost."

"Lost, huh?"

"That's right." Frank held up his cup. "On my walk yesterday. It's my favorite cup, so I waited until low tide, then walked the beach in the hopes I could find it. And voila!"

Preston took a small step back like he had smelled something offensive. "You don't think I seen you? With your binoculars? Staring at me and Carmen? Like those fucking geezers who keep coming around with that rolling cooler full of beer?"

Frank sighed. "This is tiring."

"What is?"

Frank swept his hand through the space between them. "This. We both know a certain kind of person lives on this beach. The kind like me and my husband. Just looking for a place to hide out away from the bigots of the world. Imagine my chagrin when I ended up finding one anyway."

Preston opened his mouth in a snarl, ready to interject some witty comeback that probably involved another homophobic slur. Frank moved on before he could talk. "The *other* kind is somebody running from something. Hiding from the law or debt collectors or a jealous lover. Which leaves us the third kind. Somebody who isn't running at all. Somebody who just needs a little room to work. A little space away from prying eyes."

Frank took a step forward. Felt a flush of satisfaction when Preston stepped back with his face filling with uncertainty. "We both know which one you are, don't we, Preston?"

His eyebrows drew down. "How do you know my name?"

Frank wanted to punch himself in the face for being so stupid, but he made his growl of frustration into a chuckle. "You have a good day, neighbor."

Frank waved with his coffee mug before turning back up the beach.

"So which kind are you really, *Wendall*?"

Frank smiled. It looked like both men were getting their information from the same source.

Chapter Fifteen

FRANK TURNED LEFT at Barney's walk. Into the shade of the marsh that the sun couldn't reach. Through a rank wall of humidity. All the way around to the mailbox.

Keeping up the act of the concerned neighbor, he looked inside. Pulled out a stack of damp flyers. Marched it back to their door. Behind the cover of the tall fence that hid the air conditioner, he pushed inside. Slapped the flyers on the growing stack on the counter.

Straight back to the bedroom where Frank sat on the edge of the bed to watch the Doria cottage. Picked up the binoculars he'd left on the windowsill.

He could see the beach side of the house, but not the marsh side. Shadows moving behind the windows in the dim interior. Then Carmen came out into the screened-in porch. Preston followed. Frank couldn't see any details, but by the lines of their bodies, he could tell they were agitated.

Pointing fingers and jutting jaws. An argument, but one confined to words. No violence that he could see.

He dropped the binoculars. Why was he so angry? Was

it the bruises on her arm? His own gullible ego? Preston's punchable face?

He brought the binoculars back up, but they were no longer on the porch. Or in the cottage, so far as Frank could see.

He went through the kitchen to stand by the back door. Looked down the gravel road that angled around to the north. If they went farther in that direction, Frank wouldn't see them. If they came through toward him …

And there they were. A white van — the tool of workmen and criminals alike. It surprised him to see Carmen driving. Preston sitting in the passenger's seat with his arms crossed. Staring at the window with a sour expression. Like he had just eaten an expired key lime pie.

Though they *all* tasted expired to Frank. Like somebody baked an air freshener.

He ducked back into the kitchen as they passed. Hung the binoculars around his neck. Tucked them under his shirt. Waited a slow count of sixty before leaving Barney's and heading for home.

Stan still wasn't there. Frank busied himself with a meal. Tuna salad and provolone on hoagie rolls with spicy salsa spread over them. Broiled until the cheese melted. Two of those, and a couple of Coronas while standing at the counter. Stan told him that was a good way to put all the weight back on, but before Frank could feel too guilty, he checked the freezer for ice cream.

Of course there was plenty.

A loaded sundae while watching the sun sink lower over the ocean, then he cleaned up and opened the laptop. Once it started, he went to LiveLyfe. Started a fake profile with one of the phantom email addresses from Stan's server.

Submitted his info, and LiveLyfe told him he couldn't

post anything until his account had been reviewed by a moderator. A small emoji with heart eyes popped up with a dialogue balloon over it. *Feel free to look around! Get ready to be a part of an amazing community!*

He typed Carmen's name. Sat back in surprise when there was more than one, but after a quick scan, the one he wanted was the second result returned by LiveLyfe's search. Carmen G. Doria.

He wondered what the G stood for as he clicked her profile link. Scrolled down through her posts. Grunted in disappointment when he saw the most recent entry was more than four months old. A filtered bikini image of her on a beach with the sun behind her, hair flying out from her head, and light blooming through like a fire.

The end of their pier was just inside the right side of the frame.

#FreshStartFriday

So they had been here for four months? At least?

He scrolled deeper into her past. Pictures of wine — a *lot* — and different beaches. Exotic flowers. Hill of Beans coffee. Platitudes written in overtly feminine font.

I AM STRONGER THAN THE WORLD MAKES ME OUT TO BE.

It seemed like a page he would expect from a woman between twenty and thirty-five — somebody Mo would have called a "basic white girl." Gen probably would have thrown a twenty-five-pound plate at him for it, but the threat wouldn't have kept him from saying it.

He looked at the pages she liked. Found Preston's profile empty of everything but a cartoon middle finger. *Oh no! This user hasn't posted in some time! Would you like to tag them?*

Frank sighed. "No, I would not."

A bit further down, he found she had liked a cafe in

Lake Heron, Florida. Below that, Frank saw an entry for Doria Natural Products, LLC. *Another* family business?

He opened a search window. Typed in her name, followed by *Lake Heron.*

No results about her, but Preston got an entry for a DUI arrest. That would explain an alpha wannabe like him sitting in the passenger seat while a *woman* drove. Probably couldn't believe she voted, either.

Then Frank saw the next line down where a different arrest report had him on charges of indecent exposure to a minor.

He'd heard the arguments before. A thirty-year-old man "dating" a seventeen-year-old. "But she was turning eighteen in one week, officer! Honest!"

Maybe she was. Maybe he even had her parents' blessing. Still a minor. The age of consent in Florida was eighteen. At least the state got *that* right.

Sending dick pics to high-school cheerleaders. "Those girls were all eighteen! I swear!"

Maybe, but they were still in *high school.*

How old was the man that raped Jenny? Did it matter to a dead girl if *he* was over eighteen or not? Of course not. But for some reason, it mattered to Frank.

He looked up to see the sun had set. The only light in the kitchen was the bulb over the stove, and his laptop screen. The beach outside was dark behind the window. Just a flicker of moonlight on the distant water.

Frank snapped his laptop screen closed.

Went to his room where he put on his dark tracksuit. Grabbed his pouch full of tools.

Outside to stay in the weeds at the side of the gravel road leading to Carmen's cottage. He slid his shoes off to approach barefoot, leaving the mud behind. Checked the windows and doors for sensors. Pulled out his sniffer and didn't even find a wifi signal coming from the house.

That seemed odd. But at least he could just pick the lock and be done with it.

Frank closed the door behind him. Lifted the black gaiter off his beard to breathe. Turned the low glow of his screen toward the floor to spread a little light into the room.

The *empty* room.

No furniture. Not even depressions where furniture had been. Just vacuum cleaner marks and traffic paths leading to the porch door. Deeper into the kitchen.

Frank stayed in the lanes made by crushed fibers. Stepped onto tile. Found only empty counters. A card table and matching chairs folded up and leaning against the wall under the window.

A butter knife in the sink next to an empty wine glass.

Nothing in any of the cabinets except for bleach wipes and a flyswatter.

In the closet at the end of the counter was a giant recycle bin full of wine and beer bottles. Mostly expensive whites and dark stouts.

In one bedroom, Frank found a neatly made double bed with matching cardboard box nightstands. A phone charging cable on the one in the corner.

The attached bathroom had a single bar of blue soap in the shower. Nothing on the vanity or inside the drawers. A section of floss in the trash can. A narrow linen closet full of towels and washcloths. Toilet paper, and a plastic plunger. The other bedroom was nearly identical.

The rest of the house was more of the same. Like nobody lived here. Certainly not as if somebody had been here for *months*.

His first discovery came from the screened-in porch.

The only signs of real life. Boxes full of wine. Stacked against the wall. He didn't think it was good to have them out here in the heat. Unless they weren't full of wine. He took one of the top boxes off. Looked at the label on the bottom. The same chardonnay she had brought over. It looked like more than twenty boxes.

Ten thousand dollars' worth of wine? Not counting what had already been consumed? Was it all stolen, or did they have expensive habits but not expensive tastes?

He put the box back and turned to see her easel set up next to a small table. He was hesitant to look. If he saw a picture of him — like what Freya would have made for him — he would go home and tell Stan he had to leave *right now*.

But it was just a charcoal drawing of a stormy sea. Not a very good one, he had to admit.

Back in the house, Frank stood in the front room. Looking from corner to corner. Up at the blank ceiling. He thought of the boats. Maybe there would be something on the patio on the side of the house. The doorway next to the closet in the kitchen. He went back, but when he opened it, Frank stepped into a garage instead of out onto a patio.

Wrinkled his nose at the smell. More funk from the marsh. Something vegetal and rotten. It reminded him of the nature reserve behind the gym where they had sunk Malick's body.

Even the tinge of blood he detected underneath. The metallic hint that made him drop into a crouch. Made him cautious.

In the corner next to the standard eight-foot door was a dark pile. The closer he got, the stronger the smell. He directed the screen at the pile. Black bags split by a long zipper. The reek of blood and mud and feces.

What had been in these bags?

He remembered Stan asking if they were big enough for a child.

He hooked one with his toes. Spread it out. Thought back to when he first saw the boats come to the pier. The way the load was spread between Carmen and Preston. Between the other two.

How many trips had they made? How many bags had they carried?

There were eight of them in the garage. How many more were in the van? Were they full? What were they full of?

Children?

Frank shook his head. That was a stretch. Whatever had been in these bags was probably dead by the time Preston and Carmen and company got to it, given the stench.

Doria Nature Services … or whatever they called themselves.

He couldn't wrap his head around what he'd found. The empty bags. The empty *house*. He put everything back the way he found it. Retracing his steps to erase any sign of his presence.

Frank closed the door behind him. Left the mystery for another day. Or after a late-night snack with Stan.

He picked his shoes up on the way around the corner. Didn't bother staying on the other side of the weeds.

Even over the smell of the marsh, he couldn't get the stench of the garage out of his head.

Chapter Sixteen

FRANK WOKE FROM A DREAMLESS NIGHT. Rolled over with a groan. It was as if he had gotten no sleep at all.

Carmen had said they were going out of town, but she hadn't said for how long. He staggered into the bathroom, wondering if she would be one day or many. Or if she was *ever* coming back. He stared at his reflection. Wasn't surprised to see how sad the thought of her not returning made his face.

His feet were sore from all the barefoot running he'd been doing. His jog this morning called for thick socks and running shoes. Not sprints on the beach, but gripping the gravel behind the cottages.

Loose shorts. Thin fabric with mesh up the sides. No shirt. There was no sun under the trees, but the air was close and humid. He finished tying his laces with a sigh of regret.

The house was silent as he stepped out the back door. The Spark was parked in its usual spot, so Stan was either working out on his own, or still in bed. Probably eating.

Frank didn't bother stretching or warming up. He just

held on to his water bottle and started down the lane with a nice and easy pace.

It was like running down the throat of some sinuous beast.

He was sweating less than a hundred yards into his jog, and the still air did little to cool him. Frank wondered why he kept doing this to himself. He understood that he would feel better later, but for now, it was torture.

The lane followed the coastline. Curving in toward the north. Wrapping around the marsh and making zigs and zags to match the encroaching water.

Algae covered launches with small canoes tied off to rusting cleats. A small pontoon boat next to Barney's dock that looked like nature was taking it back one slimy vine at a time.

A Partridge Pharma dinghy cut through the slick of algae on the surface as it passed. The trolling motor humming and burping behind it. Frank waved, and as usual, the intern sitting at the tiller waved back. A shaggy-haired kid with eyes still puffy from sleep.

He made a note to find out a little more about what they were doing here. The science behind the inspection of the neurotoxins found in the Playa Dolor marshes. Why *this* place?

The lane curved farther inland, and when the trees opened up, Frank was at Carmen's driveway. He continued past with a glance, but his gaze swept over another small boat puttering by. No markings, and Frank didn't recognize the man steering. Unlike the Partridge intern, the guy looked wide awake. Like he had been at this for hours already. Blond hair pulled back into a glistening ponytail. Deep tan on his neck. Sleeveless tropical shirt.

Frank waved and the man seemed not to see him, but to Frank it felt like being ignored.

The boat cut a slow arc to accelerate off in the same direction Frank was headed. The human suntan ducked under the arched walkway built over the water. Behind the boat, the disturbance in the surface vegetation made it look like the vessel had come from the narrow waterway leading to Carmen's dock.

All of his observations were adding up to something, but Frank couldn't figure out what. He just wasn't crisp. Only paying attention to what his addictions needed — dictated mostly by his body.

Food. Alcohol. And now, risky sex.

He shook his head and picked up his pace. Squirted water toward his mouth. Swallowed what he managed to get on target.

A little over two miles later, he came out from under the shade of the oak and willow trees, skidding to a halt, then squinting and bending over to catch his breath.

He drained the rest of his water. Took a slow look as he turned in a circle. Lifting his arms out to catch the breeze blowing across the clearing.

He was all the way to the RV park. The permitted lots with power and water hookups for long-term occupancy. Frank shook his head at the Stit AC truck parked in the first spot. Made a note of the other lots. The Partridge space was filled with a box truck with the rear door rolled up. Lawn chairs and awnings. A grill and several coolers. Faint music. Was it a research team or a beach party?

The university truck was next to it, and Frank had to smile. Students and young interns working in private next to a secluded beach with zero public traffic. It was *research*, all right.

He'd managed a little research of his own, so who was he to blame?

Besides, it was the next truck that interested him. The

one without any markings. Plain and dirty. Elbow to elbow with an old RV the size of a school bus. Plastic picnic table under a tattered umbrella.

Voices from the shared docs on his left made him stop his inspection. Turned with a smile as a young woman in a breezy skirt and a yellow bikini top ascended the rise next to a muscled youth with the bearing of a man used to getting what he wanted with his bleached grin.

Frank admitted that was probably unfair, but boys like that never knew what it was like to work for it.

The kids saw him, and both waved. He was sure everyone around here knew about him and Stan — or at least knew what they were *supposed* to. It gave Frank an idea as he waved back. Before they could get close enough to stop him with some neighborly conversation, he broke into an easy jog, ducking back under the cover of the trees. Set an easy pace for the return trip.

At the small bridge leading to Carmen's, he slowed to take the turn like it had been his destination the whole time. He had no excuse ready if he was caught running up to the cottage. He would just act like he didn't know his neighbors were gone.

It didn't matter. There was nothing more to see. Just the same boardwalks and choking algae. The dock behind the house was in nice repair, though. Maintained and painted. Just like the pier.

He puzzled at that observation on his way back. Cut into the brown grass in the backyard. Kicked through some black mulch that smelled like wet farts. To the small shed in the back corner, where Frank found the first locked door on the property. A stack of blue kiddie pools leaned against the lee side of the shed. Against a window that was so dirty with a caked layer of moss, he couldn't see inside.

He didn't bother hiding his confusion as he left the

property. Turned to jog past Barney's place. Looking up to find himself home without remembering the last part of the run.

This mystery would require more digging. He hoped Carmen came back soon. He had some questions for her, and he hoped … the memory of her throwing her head back flashed in his mind … the feel of her skin under his fingers.

He burned the image away with a wash of shame. He should be looking for Jenny's killer. He should be finding out more about Owens and his plans. He should be punching Ty Kirby in his smug face. Any number of things worth more than what happened to his penis.

Then he thought of the bruises on Carmen's arms. The anger in her voice when she tried to tell him about what Preston was forcing her to do.

He looked up at the back door of the house he shared with his cousin. His fake husband. They just now got the safe internet. The ability to communicate outside of their exile. The old investigation could now continue, but there was no reason to let this new one go. Especially if it meant he might see Carmen again.

See Carmen again … he rolled his eyes at himself. He knew what he really wanted from her. And maybe she even wanted it from *him*. Or she was playing him like he and Stan suspected.

Did it matter?

Frank was breathing heavily. Not just from exertion, but from frustration. He knew what he was going to do. He had an absolute *certainty* in mind. Why bother arguing?

He would ease back into the Pedophile Junction investigation as soon as he got to the bottom of what was happening with Carmen and Preston Doria. The opportu-

nity to take care of a man he *knew* was an abuser at least —
a criminal at worst. A terrible man.

That was his job. And could anybody really fault him
for finding a little joy in another human's body?

That sounded exactly like the argument he used when
first deciding to cheat on Sarah. But he wasn't *cheating* this
time. At least, not on anybody else. Only himself.

For some reason, that made him feel better.

Chapter Seventeen

STAN LOOKED DOWN at the note Frank slid across the table. He set his fork on the edge of the plate. Wiped his napkin across his mouth, but instead of removing the trail of syrup from his chin, he smeared it into a glistening ink blot.

"What's this?"

"A shopping list."

Stan looked up over the edge of the paper. "Steak and crab? What're we doing here?"

Frank shrugged as he cut into his stack of pancakes. "I just thought we could do a seafood boil. Or a cookout."

"For how many people? This is a lot."

Frank told him about his morning jog. The unsavory boatman. The RV park. The coeds feigning research. "I say we have a little grill session in the gravel at the end of the lane. There's a break in the trees with a nice breeze coming off the ocean. Utility hookups—"

Stan slapped the note on the table. "Yeah, I been there. In fact, I *own* it."

"Then you know how nice it could be to have a little party over there."

Stan leaned back and crossed his arms. "What are you doing? We need to start making plans to move our operation to a more … to somewhere with less distractions. Where we can try to stay under the radar. I mean, I thought this was a pretty good place, but then you started fucking the neighbors—"

"I'm not— It was just *one* neighbor."

Stan grinned. Frank had to admit to himself how ridiculous that sounded. Realized Stan was just taking a shot.

"Look," Frank said. "Something is rotten around here."

"Yeah, it's the algae."

"Static, please."

At the sound of his military nickname, Stan sobered immediately. Leaned forward to put his elbows on the table. "How important is this to you?"

Frank shook his head. "I don't know. I just know something is making me itch between my shoulder blades. Right where I can't reach."

"Do you think the girl is in danger?"

"Yes." Then Frank sighed in frustration. "No … I don't know."

"What's going on, Frank?"

Frank looked up at the ceiling. "Something is happening here. The Dorias are up to something. They have an obvious accomplice—"

"Or competitor."

Frank hadn't thought of that. He looked back to Stan and lifted a finger to concede the point. "Or competitor, yes. But competing in what?"

"So, the cookout is part of the investigation? Ask the kids what's up? Probably get gossip about who's banging who. Hell, maybe *you're* on that list."

"Come on."

Stan put his hands up. "That was the last one. I swear."

Frank started back in on his pancakes. "We'll see. Anyway, since I have put us in jeopardy with my behavior, I want to take our remaining time to investigate this itch."

Stan laughed. "Do you realize how that sounds?"

"I do."

Stan waved his hand at him before going back. "Look, that little red-headed gal seeing your search was … unfortunate. But it wasn't your fault. You hadn't boffed her yet, and it was a residual bad habit that let her see the screen in the first place."

Frank looked up at him from under his brows. "Boffed?"

"Would you like something more colorful?"

"Yes. I think I would. But without the f-word, please."

"Fine. This was before you and her did the dance of the dirty frog."

"I don't know if that's better."

Stan sighed. "It's just timing, Frank. Coupled with our inherent self-destructive behavior. It pushes up our schedule a bit, but it's honestly not that big a deal. I need about two weeks to set something else up anyway. I mean, that's what was *gonna* happen anyway. This was just a place to heal up and relax. We were both going stir crazy, and to be honest, as far as a little action goes, I ain't surprised you fit it in."

Frank snorted laughter. "You realize how *that* last part sounded?"

"I do."

Frank sopped up the remaining drizzle of syrup with the last bite of pancake. "I don't think discovering the name of your Galveston company was a problem. Yes, if I could do it, it shows that *somebody* could."

Stan nodded. "It shows a weakness in my planning. Something we'll need to look out for the next time."

Frank pushed his plate away. Slid his coffee cup closer for a sip. "Carmen seeing the search box with her name in it was just *very* unlucky. At a time when I didn't even know the significance."

"Something in all likelihood that wouldn't have made you look as deep if it hadn't been for her seeing it in the first place."

"Correct. *But*, she *did* see it. And I *did* find out your little secret."

"Right. And you *did* boff her."

"Even though I was certainly there, I think *she* did the boffing."

"No, you don't get to do that." Stan shook his head. "Like those cheating assholes who talk about some chick just started sucking their dick. What were they supposed to do?"

"That's not what I meant."

"Then what *did* you mean? It's not like your dick popped out — fully hard and ready to go — and she just *fell* on it. *WHOOPSIE!* And she just *kept* falling on it for a minute and a half?"

"It was longer than a minute and a half."

"You should be so lucky, old man. That's not the fucking point."

Frank raised his right hand. "Is there anything connecting your real name to the Stit AC company? Or to Arthur and Macy Daniels?"

"Not directly, no. But secrets are more powerful when less people know them."

"Fewer."

Stan leaned over his plate and pointed at the center of

Frank's face. "Stop that shit. *Fewer*, okay? The fewer people that know a thing, the better the secret."

Frank stood to gather the breakfast dishes. "Fine. So how long do we have?"

"We just have to make sure we don't leave a trail of crumbs when we go out to Wildwood."

Frank paused halfway to the sink. "To Mo and Gen's place?"

"Oh yeah."

"I didn't know that was the plan."

"You've been kind of a mopey bitch. Hard to have a conversation with."

Frank wanted to argue, but Stan was right. He had been deflecting and blaming and ignoring. He knew it wasn't right. Not even deep down. He knew it right on the surface.

When they first got here, he kept his shame hidden, but now it was plain as day.

He sighed as he took the last few steps to the counter. "I'm sorry, Stan."

"Well, I haven't been a ray of sunshine myself. But in my defense, you've been annoying the absolute shit outta me."

Frank still couldn't disagree. He hung his head while filling the sink. He felt Stan's hand on his shoulder and chuckled. "We *are* like a married gay couple."

Stan didn't laugh. Instead, he made his hand into a fist. Began beating a gentle rhythm. That calming heartbeat that had pulled him out of previous panic attacks. "I'll tell you what, Frank. You got serious problems. Shit that a doctor needs to dig into. It fucking breaks my heart — every time I see you go out and hurt yourself. Even when it comes back on me, it goes through you first. I wish you knew that you didn't have to do it. That you don't have to punish yourself."

Frank pulled away from his touch. "What are you talking about?"

"Jesus, Frank. How long is it gonna take?"

"What?"

"Before you realize that it wasn't your fault."

The soapy plate slipped from Frank's fingers. Splashed suds up onto his arm. "But it was. All of it."

"You killed your daughter?"

"I didn't stop it."

"How could you have?"

"I killed Sarah."

"The *fuck* you did. She killed herself."

"Because of me."

"Because her daughter had been raped and murdered."

"Because her husband abandoned her."

"Oh, for fuck's sake. She did what you don't have the balls to do."

Frank spun to face him. "*That's* courage?"

Stan shook his head. "I wonder something. Did it hurt so bad because you lost her, or because you didn't have anybody to take it out on anymore?"

"What do you know about it? What have you *ever* lost?"

Stan smiled. Looked away. "I lost plenty. Don't ever fucking think otherwise. But the thing that hurts right now? I'm losing you."

Frank shocked himself by laughing. A burst of sound that erupted like a sneeze. He bent over. Looked up at Stan's confusion, only to laugh harder.

Then realization dawned on Stan's face. "Holy shit. We *are* an old married couple."

Frank nodded and wiped tears from his eyes. "That

could have been in a movie-of-the-week. The only thing missing was a group hug."

Stan went back to the table to slump down in his chair. "Did we even resolve anything?"

"I don't think so."

Stan picked up Frank's cookout wish list. "Well, Wendall dear. As soon as you finish the dishes, how would you like to go shopping?"

Frank dried his hands before covering his heart. "I would love nothing more, Trevor darling."

"There gonna be beer at this cookout?"

Frank rolled his eyes as he turned back to the dishes. "Since you're paying for it, absolutely."

Stan sighed. "I'm paying for everything lately."

Funny. That's exactly how Frank felt.

Chapter Eighteen

FRANK WAS surprised by how excited Stan became about the cookout. Like he was planning a party for a buddy's retirement. Chattering away all the way home from the store.

Coolers packed full of food and drinks on ice. Making the Chevy Spark dip on its suspension.

There were small grills mounted on poles down at the park, but Stan said, "Fuck that. I'll tie ours to the back of the Spark with a bungee if I have to."

They packed like they were going away for the weekend, filling the back of the car until the hatch wouldn't close. True to his word, Stan rigged the grill so it could be pulled behind them. He used a nylon tow strap instead of a bungee, and Frank still couldn't help staring at it with crossed arms. Shaking his head.

"What?" Stan stopped to spread his hands. "You wanna push the fucker the whole way there? Bitch?"

"Who, me?" Frank touched his chest and gave an innocent smile. "No, I'm only admiring your ingenuity. A negative thought never crossed my mind."

"Didn't think so. Is there anything else we need?"

"I can't imagine what it might be."

Stan looked at the bulging load. Lifted his shoulders in a guilty shrug. "Okay, maybe I went a little overboard, but it was *your* idea."

Frank pointed at the car. "I don't think *that* was my idea."

"Well, in for a dollar," Stan said.

"Don't you mean a penny?"

Stan grinned as he dropped into the driver's seat. "Not with as much as we spent, no."

They headed down the gravel lane toward the RV park at a slow enough pace to keep the grill from tipping over, Frank watching the trees creep by with a mixed feeling of guilt and anticipation.

Looking deeper into the emotion, he realized it was how he'd been feeling for weeks. Knowing what he was *supposed* to be doing, but creating an unrelated task list in his mind. Then convincing himself it was too important to ignore. So he could disregard what was *truly* important. Give himself with an escape hatch excuse.

What a complicated way to avoid responsibility.

"What was that about?" Stan said.

"What was *what* about?"

The lane opened into the lot with the utility slots for RVs. Stan steered toward the opening in the trees leading to ocean. Parked and turned to look at Frank. "That sigh you just blew out. It was pretty dramatic."

Frank grinned. "I didn't even realize I had made any noise, let alone a dramatic sigh."

Stan drummed his fingers on the wheel. "Look, I know this is frivolous. But the underlying reason is sound. This is a good way to get some info about our neighbors. Probably something we shoulda done a long time ago. Even though this is probably a time to buckle down, I can't blame you for being distracted. Shit, I spent *years* not looking into my own behavior. With all my talk about therapy, I can't really fault you too much. So let's do this. Let's play the merry couple. Cook this food and drink this beer, and if the kids ain't around to eat, I'll make lobster mac and cheese with the leftovers for a week."

Neither of them should have worried. Barely fifteen minutes had passed before there was any interest. And just as Frank had suspected, most of them were barely past an age that he would have still described as *children*.

But one of the older ones was Isaac, an engineer about Frank's age who said he was there to fix the RV and lab equipment — then he leaned in with a wink. "I'm mostly here as a mature eye on the situation, but little does Partridge know, I'm actually a bad influence."

A black couple from the university, new-age types with matching clothes and matching hair — wild fros, loose shorts under oversized shirts, and sneakers so white, they seemed to glow like the reflective markers on the highway. Their names were Pat and Marion, and though Frank was fairly certain the couple had one of each gender, the names didn't help him figure out which was which.

He was saved further struggle by a party breaking out. Like he and Stan had performed a magic trick. Just add water, and *POOF!*

Music. Folding chairs. Cornhole. More beer of the poor college student variety — Frank did his best not to sneer — and Jell-O shots. Two blondes wearing practically nothing brought them all lined up on two cookie sheets.

When the smell of weed blew overhead in a cloud, Frank wasn't shocked.

Frank spent a dizzying few minutes on introductions — names he knew he wouldn't remember — before finding his way back to the grill where Isaac and Stan were deep in a discussion about smoking pork. No less than five young men complimented Frank on his beard, and he was slightly bothered by how good each one made him feel.

Standing in the billow of smoke rolling over from the grill made him feel better. Like he could finally hide. Talking to Isaac taught him how wrong he was about the party, though. This was nothing special.

Except for the occasional audit, where he and the interns washed up and put everything in order, they were out here with no corporate supervision. Properly filled out forms and official correspondence with a regular shipment of de-watered algae for the labs to dig through, and it was a prolonged vacation.

As far as the university was concerned, Pat and Marion had a similar system. They lived in near-independence every summer, watched over the critical research that would give their students plenty of credits toward their degrees, and as long as the paperwork was correct for the school to show to the oversight committee, it was almost perfect.

If only the algae wasn't toxic.

But there was beach access, and so long as they avoided the churning dunes of silica, they were fine.

Frank realized they had made a small community. A perpetual summer of love staffed by kids far too smart for their own good. Easy and free with each other — and why wouldn't they be? Arguments and intellectual clashes jeopardized their little utopia.

It bordered on amazement, and Frank wondered what he would have done with the opportunity if it had been offered forty years ago. He smiled to himself. He probably would have reported them.

Neither one of them had really asked what they would

do if nobody showed up. It was like the "Field of Dreams" of barbecues.

Frank sat back like a bemused grandparent. Content to watch for a while before wading in for answers. When he saw the tan-master from this morning join in on a game of Frisbee golf that sent his first disc dangerously close to the swamp's murky shoreline, Frank watched him while trying not to *look* like he was watching.

The same shirt as before. Tight ponytail looking freshly oiled. He had the same youthful bearing as the interns and students, but with a shifty demeanor. Like he was looking for an opening. Frank wondered what the opening was for.

Sex? Drugs?

Then a phone came out of his pocket. He signaled for a pause with an upheld finger. Put the phone to his ear. Nodded. Gave an irritated sneer of a smile as he hung up. Trotted to the rusty RV with the tattered awning.

The golf game continued without him as he entered the RV. Frank could hear the springs on the door squeal from all the way across the lot.

Then the crunching of tires over gravel, and the Dorias' white van slid by. The party split around it like water peeling away from the sides of a boat. The sun glared off the driver's window.

The van pulled into the spot on the far side of the RV. Tan Man rushed back out of the side door, followed by a large man with even darker skin. Wispy hair, almost white, an angry red scalp showing through.

Tan Man and Red Head disappeared behind the RV, and Frank heard the metal cargo doors slamming closed. They were either loading or unloading something from the van. He waited, but instead of Tan Man and Red Head coming back around the side, they went to the rear of the

RV — a school bus in its previous life, so they were at the emergency exit.

Frank could see the edge of what they were doing. Putting something into the back of the converted RV. So they had *unloaded* the van.

Was it bodies? Money? More wine?

Frank glanced at Stan. Saw how his cousin was watching over Isaac's shoulder. Frank nodded before turning back. Starting a casual stroll that would take him to a foursome of kids at a plastic card table. Closer, he saw they weren't playing poker or euchre, or *any* card game he was familiar with. Colorful pictures of spirits and warriors.

He was instantly bored, but feigned an interested smile as he stepped up behind the shoulder of another observer and said, "This is definitely not Bridge."

The kid he had sneaked up on flinched away, startled. A nervous laugh snorted from his sunburned nose. "Oh shit!"

Frank chuckled. Held up a hand in apology. "Sorry about that."

The kid shook his head. "No, I was just caught up in the turn."

Frank leaned forward politely. "The turn?"

The kid pointed at the table where he and Frank were being ignored in favor of the flip of every card. "Yeah, this is the Diamond Rush expansion pack."

The kid turned away like that had explained everything, but before Frank could ask for a *bit* more information, Carmen walked out from around the RV.

A yawn and a stretch that pulled the bottom of her tee to show her pale belly button. The red coils of her hair bounced away and around her arms.

Frank stepped around the card table. Glanced back at the startled nerd. "Make sure you kids get some food."

He heard them mutter behind them. Something about how *he* was one of the guys that had started this impromptu party. He wouldn't have minded taking a moment to turn that revelation toward his advantage — pumping them for information — but he couldn't take his attention off of Carmen as she turned around the front of the RV and noticed him staring.

He was afraid she would snarl in disgust. Or hesitate before smiling back, but her immediate grin eased his worry. She waved, then jumped into a prancing jog that brought her close enough for him to see the sunlight bouncing off the water behind him reflecting off the lenses of her sunglasses.

Chapter Nineteen

CARMEN TOOK FRANK'S BEER, her fingers holding the contact against his for a moment before bringing the bottle to her lips. As she tipped her head back, he could see bruising around her left eye. A shocking contrast of ugly color.

He clenched his teeth. Forced a smile as she finished the final few swallows. Let the bottle dangle against her thigh as she turned to put her arm around his waist. "This is not how I expected to see you."

"Where's Preston?"

She looked away with a sigh of exasperation. Steered him through the kids standing in social clumps. Headed toward the grill where Frank could tell Stan was watching through the smoke.

"Not what I expected at all," Carmen said.

He'd let her avoid the question for now. "What *did* you expect?"

She looked up at him with a fresh grin. "Maybe more of a hope than an expectation."

"Oh yeah?"

She shrugged. "Like maybe on the pier again? That was nice."

Isaac turned and caught sight of her before Frank could respond. "Miss Carmen!"

Her grin faded. She pulled Frank to a stop. "That man is a lecherous pervert."

Frank nodded. "Most men are."

"Not you. The only man who hasn't spent his time ogling me. Or taking advantage of me. The only man that's been honest."

Frank thought about the times he spent looking at her through the binoculars. The fantasies he had about her that he gladly fulfilled in spite of how wrong it was to have sex with a married woman. Compromising her. *Lying* to her. He said a silent prayer of gratitude that his skin was dark enough to hide his shame. "I haven't been honest with you at all."

She flapped her hand. Then slapped him on the shoulder. "Maybe you haven't been honest with *yourself* — or *Trevor* — but I can tell when a man is into me."

"I'd like to be into you again."

She threw her head back and laughed. Throaty and musical, the free and open sound of it burning his embarrassment away. He couldn't believe he'd said that.

"Oh my," she said, waving air into her face.

"What's so funny?" Stan's voice from behind him.

Frank turned to find him a few steps away, standing with a bemused smile. The greasy spatula held out to the side with his elbow almost touching his hip. Stan stepped in and kissed him on the cheek before he could answer.

Frank saw Isaac's mouth twist in disgust. Couldn't deal with a man giving another man a tiny peck on the cheek? Another one for Frank to put on a list of people he didn't like.

Frank shifted his attention back to his cousin. "This is Carmen Doria."

She kept a hold of Frank's waist. Held her hand out. "And you must be Trevor Scott. Wendall has told me almost *nothing* about you."

Stan took her hand. "He's told me *everything* about *you*."

One side of her mouth quirked up. "Has he now?" She finally dropped her arm and stepped to the side and looked up at Frank with that same smile. "See, honesty."

Frank forced his gaze away. Waved toward the grill. "I'm starving."

Stan grinned. "I have a plate all set aside for you."

Frank nodded, then pointed at Isaac's departing back. "Where's your friend going?"

Stan puckered his mouth like he'd tasted something sour. "That man is not my friend. In fact, he's a fucking asshole."

Carmen laughed again, and Frank made himself a promise to make her laugh as often as possible. "That has been *my* opinion of him, as well."

Stan turned back to walk around the grill. "I wonder how many of these lovely young ladies he's been creeping on." He pointed at Frank with his spatula. "Some of these girls are *smart*. I'm talking engineers and scientists and shit. To think somebody would reduce them to nothing but …" his gaze flickered over to regard Carmen. "Well, you know."

Carmen followed him around the grill to dig into the cooler behind his knees. Pulled out two bottles. "I *do* know, believe it or not."

Stan sent Frank a mischievous grin. "With a body like yours, I can imagine. My Wendall has been quite taken by it. Always a sucker for what he calls the *thick chicks*."

Frank came a hair's breadth from blurting Stan's real name in outrage. Cleared his throat. "Trevor!"

Stan waved at the parking lot to indicate the young bodies. "I mean, look at some of them. It looks like a summer movie set. A coming-of-age sex comedy. Or the prologue to a porno."

Carmen handed Frank the opened bottle of beer. Her lips were pressed into a thin line, and her face was turning red. At first, he thought she was angry, then he realized she was trying not to laugh. He sighed. "If I didn't know better, I'd think you two were teaming up on me."

Stan gasped in mock offense. "Why Wendall darling, how could you ever?"

Carmen lost her hold on the laughter, and Frank took a moment to enjoy the sound. She sniffed and lifted her sunglasses enough to wipe her eyes. He noticed the sclera of the bruised eye was dark red and bloodshot.

He took a long drink to keep from growling with rage.

Carmen set her glasses back on her nose and turned to Stan. "Trevor, I'd like to borrow Wendall for a moment. May I?"

Stan batted his lashes at her before answering. "Just save some for me, sweetie."

Frank barely heard. Let her take his hand and pull him away from the grill. He was distracted by a gnawing question. Had he ever told her Stan's fake name? And she also knew their fake last name. Had he told her that too?

"Did you really tell him about us?" Carmen had led him to the thin trail that would take them to the beach. Into the wind stream that brought the marsh to his nose.

"Of course I did. But the details are ours."

She shook her head. "Do you realize how sweet what you just said was?"

"To be honest, no."

She stopped. Looked around like she was checking for observers. "That's why it *is*. You are a romantic, Wendall. And I have thought a lot about you."

"I've thought a lot about you too."

She leaned to the side to look down the beach. Frank pulled her back. "Are you looking for Preston?" He pointed at her eye. "Afraid he'll do it again? Or something worse?"

She pulled back with a smile. Touched her cheek under the black eye. "This? It's nothing. I fell down and hit the corner of the coffee table."

"That's the exact thing many abused women say."

She sighed. Threw her head back to make her hair bounce. "You sound like a cop."

"Do you want me to talk to him?"

She put her hands on her hips. "And say what?"

Frank bared his teeth. "There would actually be very little to say."

Her mouth fell open. "Are you serious? You would *talk* to Preston? Because you think … because he's hitting me?"

Frank took her hand. He didn't know where his passion was coming from. Couldn't figure out what was making him act like a jealous lover. Like some knight preparing to rescue a damsel that never asked for it. He wanted to stop such nonsense, but the harder he tried to calm himself, the hotter his anger became.

"I want you to live as free as I know you deserve."

Carmen licked her lips. "That is … I said it before. No man has said anything like that to me. *Ever*. Or made me feel like this."

"Like what?"

"Like letting you drag me into the weeds and doing whatever you wanted to me. Like doing whatever I wanted to *you*."

He took a step back and swallowed. Shook his head.

"No. I don't want your body as a reward. I don't want to—"

"Jesus Christ, that's not what I'm talking about!"

They both looked up and down the trail, but there was no one to overhear. Or stop them.

"Are you going to come back and have something to eat?" He had to stop himself.

Her face fell slack into confusion. "What?" her voice was barely above a whisper.

"I should get back."

She tipped her head. Like she was listening for a distant voice. "So do I."

She turned toward the beach and marched off.

Frank watched her all the way to the sand, where she finally looked back. He couldn't see her face, but her gait became more relaxed after seeing him. Like Carmen had been worried that she'd look back to find him gone.

Almost as worried as Frank was that she wouldn't turn back at all.

He heard voices. Some of the kids coming down from the RV park. Turned toward them so he wouldn't be caught staring after her by anyone who might talk. But what did it really matter? He had handled this whole thing so poorly.

He and Stan should go. They should head out to the next "safe" location without looking back. But he wanted to see her again. And maybe talk to Preston. Just a quick chat before leaving.

He lifted his beer for a drink, but realized it was empty. He didn't remember drinking it.

Chapter Twenty

BY THE TIME they got back to the house, Frank was struggling to keep his words straight. Speaking slowly and with purpose. He could feel his forehead wrinkling in concentration.

He got out of the car before Stan had come to a complete stop. Smiled and waved at an imaginary crowd to let them know he was okay. Made his way back to the rear to help Stan get the grill back to the patio.

Stan loosened the toe strap. Stood up to lean on the grill with his elbows planted on the greasy lid. "Did you know this marsh is actually freshwater?"

Frank tried to work moisture into his mouth. He'd have to drink a couple bottles of water before bed if he didn't want to wake up with a dehydration headache. "Nope. Didn't know that. Is that good or bad?"

Stan shrugged before going back to pulling the grill through the gravel. "Fuck if I know, but the nerds all thought it was amazing."

Frank lifted his end of the grill. Banged his shins

against the shelf along the bottom. Stumbled with a hissing curse.

Stan looked back with a chuckle. "Yeah, it turns out I bought an ecological oddity, and only the recalcitrant nature of my assumed identity as Mr. and Mrs. Daniels that keeps it a fairly guarded option for research."

"None of what we saw today was research. And recalcitrant is a pretty good word."

"Yeah, I like it."

They heaved the grill into its final position. Turned back to unload the rest. A much smaller task than it had been at the start of the cookout. The day had laid waste to their purchases. The pile next to the grill when they were done signified they had both decided to clean everything up and bring it inside tomorrow.

Stan lowered into a cushioned chair with a soft groan. Reached up with one hand to rub at the scar on his shoulder while reaching into the cooler with the other one to fish out one of the few remaining beers. Passed one to Frank before opening his own. "What are we doing here, Frank?"

He took a long swallow from a beer he didn't need. Sighed as he sat on the ground. "I don't know anymore."

Stan took half the beer in a noisy guzzle. Leaned back to belch behind his hand. "Jesus, did we ever?"

Frank closed his eyes. Saw Sarah's face appear out of the black of his imagination. Watched it dissolve into wavering fog. The smoky color shifted to red. Became Carmen's bouncing coils. Her weathered face. That wry smile.

He could see Jenny over his shoulder. She was running. But not AWAY from something. It had more purpose. Like somebody at play. Then he saw Freya join her. Running alongside her.

Then Rory Day.

And all of their faces were full of smiling joy.

He heard their laughter. Amplified by more voices as more and more girls came into view. All running and laughing. A swirling circle in a bright field.

He wanted to join them. Be as free as them. He felt a hand in his, and he was terrified to look. He didn't want to know who was there. If it was Sarah, he would want it to be Carmen instead. If it was Carmen, he would curse himself for being disrespectful to a good woman's memory.

Frank opened his eyes. Wiped the dribble of snot from his mustache. Let the tears fall. "I thought I wanted to be better."

Stan sat forward. The bottle dangled between his knees. "Better what?"

Frank shrugged and looked into the darkness of the marsh. "It's too late to be a better father."

"Frank … come on."

"But it is. It doesn't matter if I'm right or wrong about damning her to death because I couldn't do enough fast enough to save her. Or if I drove my wife to kill herself. Or any of that. What matters is the truth of what I just said. It's too late to be a better father. A better husband. I'm too old to start over. Too old to see if I still have it in me."

"I don't know if that's true at all."

Frank finished the rest of his beer. Tossed the bottle over the rail. It hummed as it spun into the dark. A fat plop as it hit the algae cover on the surface. A bubbling gurgle as it sank.

His mind flashed on the vision of Malick's body. Its face a mask of torn flesh and blood. Rotating under to hide the features under the water as it sank with wet fart bubbles. He snorted a bitter chuckle. Wiped his eyes. "You're a young man still. It doesn't matter how old you feel, as long as you don't succeed in killing yourself by eating like a trash can, you got plenty of time left."

"I got no plans for self-improvement anyway."

"Stan, you're not listening to me. I said nothing about volition. I said there was no time for me. Nothing left. Nothing but the feeling. Whatever can overcome the numbness that is slowly shutting my mind down. I can't think about anything but the next time."

"The next time for what?"

He saw Carmen astride him. Felt the heat of her breath on his face. Wondered why he couldn't stop thinking about her. Then he thought about the feel of the gun in his hand. The sight of Patrick Dahl's blood spreading across his living room floor. Malick Briar looking up in horror as the gun pointed at his chest.

Then he imagined Detective Owens in front of him. Both of them pointing guns. Both of them ready to fire.

Frank sighed. "It's even too late for me to be a better cop. The only thing I can really be is worse."

"Maybe I'm dumber than I think. Worse at what?"

"No, buddy. You are exactly as dumb as you think."

Stan laughed. Shook his head as he drained his beer. "That still doesn't answer me."

Frank struggled to his feet. Steadied himself against the grill. "I'm none of those things still. I'm not a father or a husband or a cop. I got nothing left to be better at."

"You can be a better man."

"But I've never just been a man. I've always been a man and one of those other things. I'm lost. I've fallen so deep into my misery that I can't remember what put me here in the first place. I'm a beating heart, but there's nothing to pump."

"Okay, maybe I'm drunker than I think too. I don't know what that means."

"I'm navigating waters without a compass. In a maze with nowhere to turn. Solving a mystery without any clues. Pick a metaphor."

"Aren't those similes?"

"Maybe, but that's all I got anyway. My figure-of-speech well ran dry."

He could just make out the sparkle in Stan's eyes as they stared at each other. Then they burst out laughing.

Stan stood with a shake of his head. "I don't know what to tell you, buddy. I'm on this ride right along with you. Just hoping it hits a brick wall."

Frank choked off his laughter. "Maybe, but you don't want it to end all at once like that, do you?"

Stan said nothing, but he looked down at his hands as they tightened into fists.

"No," Frank continued. "We're too much alike. You don't want it to be quick and painless. You want it to hurt."

"It's the only thing I can still feel," Stan whispered, then turned and shuffled inside. Banged his shoulder off the door jamb and cursed under his breath.

Frank put his back to the house. Peered into the deep black of the hanging willow limbs. The bare glitter of stars on the ocean out at the edge of his vision. He heard a splash. A ripple. Like some sinuous creature slipped by on the surface of the marsh. A large snake or an alligator. Something big enough to swallow a man.

The smell was rotten and sharp. Worse in the night without the breeze coming off the tide. The still air trapping the funk a few feet from the ground. Wet earth and blood. Feces and spoiled meat. Much like what he had smelled in Carmen's garage.

But less pungent. The potency lost in the diffusion of being outside the small building.

The odor reminded him of the white van. Made him

think about the tanned boatman motoring out of the bend in front of Carmen's house. It made that unreachable spot in the center of his back itch something fierce. It was a thread to pick at. Something to pull that would unravel the question to reveal the answer.

Or another clue.

It was like pushing on a bruise. Massaging a swollen joint.

Frank needed a fix. Some kind of satisfaction. He thought of the black ring around Carmen's eye. Felt the anger and outrage boil up from his gut. He needed to know what they had been doing that night he first saw them. He needed to know what Tan Man and Red Head were doing behind Carmen's van. He needed to know if she was serious about him.

Or was she really playing him? And if she was, what was she playing for?

He sat on the patio couch. Fell over and stretched out. Began to fall asleep to the sound of the night bugs. Like they were trying to tell him something, and he just too exhausted to hear what they were saying.

Chapter Twenty-One

FRANK WOKE up with a spear of sunlight dancing across his eyelids. A bit of blue sky bouncing above him, revealed through the fluttering leaves.

His mouth was dry and swollen. His eyes felt like they were crusted with salt.

He was in the same position he had fallen asleep in, with his joints now on fire. His lower back ached with his pounding heartbeat. If killing himself with alcoholic liver disease was his goal, he was right on track.

Rising into a sitting position made his head explode with pain. He gritted his teeth and looked out of a single squinted eye as he forced himself to stand. It took several steps toward the back door before he was walking a straight line.

He forced his posture straight. Shoulders back and head erect. Grunted against the insistence of his full bladder. He flung the door open and gasped as the cool air hit his sweaty face. Assaulted by the thick smell of bacon.

Stan turned with his eyebrows raised. "You look like a bag of melted shit."

Frank waved him off as he passed through the kitchen.

Stan leaned out past the edge of the counter. "We're gonna talk later. Some serious shit for both of us."

"That sounds fantastic," Frank muttered.

"I heard that!"

Frank made it to his bathroom without dribbling urine down his leg. Like an old man at a nursing home. He kicked off his sandals. Got out of his shorts and stood over his stream while pulling his shirt off. After a shiver hit that almost made him pee on the edge of the bowl, he went to the sink to splash water on his face and head. He drank his fill of the chlorine-tinged supply. Brushed his teeth twice. Finished with a careful combing of his tangled beard before donning his running shorts.

He was going to get his sprint in. Instead of habit or necessity, Frank would do it as punishment.

Stan watched him from over his heaping plate of eggs and bacon in the kitchen. A knowing smirk.

Frank put ice in his stainless-steel canteen. Filled it with cold water. Saluted his cousin on his way out.

"Proud of you, buddy," Stan said.

"Maybe you should join me, fat boy."

"First off — ow! Second — work out on a full stomach? In this heat?"

Frank let the screen door slam behind him.

He felt far from normal when he started his sprints. Far worse than normal when he finished. He'd barely spared a glance at the Doria place. Spared no thought for anything more than the fear that this time he was actually going to die.

The cold water made him cramp up, but the pure bliss of it in his mouth made everything better. A drizzle across his forehead. Down his back to make him shiver under the blazing sun.

His breath was back by the time he reached his little boardwalk leading into the shade, and as he stepped out of the sun, Frank had to admit feeling a bit of pride in himself. A man his age doing that much work? After a good drunk?

He suspected most men half his age couldn't have kept up. Then his smug satisfaction turned sour when he looked up to see Carmen leaning out over the railing of his side porch. Watching him with her knowing half-smile.

The same dancing shaft of sunlight that had burned into his sleep had moved across the boards to hit her head like a blazing halo. Like her red hair was made of actual flames. Arms crossed under her breasts. The fabric of her tank top pulled tight across her chest.

Frank nodded as he neared her. Turned into the opening in the railing. She looked back at him over her shoulder. Her denim shorts were even shorter than the last ones, showing the crease at the top of her hamstring. One bare foot planted back on the toes, the sole blackened with dirt.

It made him think of wild freedom. Something he would have never seen as attractive. Maybe it was because he was falling for her. Annoyances suddenly made cute by infatuation.

He looked away like he had been caught staring at a stranger. "Good morning, neighbor."

She turned and leaned back with her elbows in the railing. Pulling the shirt even tighter. "It doesn't look so good for you, neighbor. Trevor told me to speak quietly."

"Thank you, but I'm fine." Frank shook his head, hating that she was here at his worst. Then he wondered just how good his best could really be.

She tipped her head like she was conceding a point.

"I'm sure you are." She stood up straight and looked down. "In fact, I know you are."

Frank wanted to go inside where it was cool. And safe. Take a shower and eat and clear his mind of the heat and confusion building up from her presence. She made it difficult to think clearly. "Is there something wrong?"

She shook her head. "I just need to talk to somebody."

"What about Preston?"

"He wouldn't understand."

"That's not what I meant."

She looked at him through narrowed eyes. "Then what? Are you afraid he'll know I'm here?"

Frank chuckled. "I told you once. I'm not afraid of him."

"Maybe you should be."

He shrugged. "Maybe."

She sighed. "He's away. Making a delivery."

Frank knew it wasn't time to ask what he was delivering. He waited in silence instead. She seemed flustered by his reaction. She tossed her head back to bounce the hair away from her face. "I just need to talk to someone who will understand."

Frank spread his hands. "I'm sorry, but I need to take a shower. There's no way I could concentrate on what you were saying if I was worried about you smelling me every time you took a breath."

She shrugged. "I don't mind."

"That's a very grounded attitude, but I still need to clean up a little."

"I'll wait."

He was pleased she was willing to wait for him. Also frustrated that he would have to hurry. He smiled and gave her a gracious nod. "I won't be long. Then maybe we could have breakfast?"

"I would like that, neighbor."

"Then I'll see you soon."

Frank went inside. Straight to his bedroom where he stripped down and started the shower. Then he pulled up before stepping into the spray. Cursed himself for being so rude. He should have offered to let her wait inside where it was cool.

He reached for a towel. Hesitated. Thought better of that in favor of throwing his shorts back on. Turned back to the bedroom to discover his offer didn't matter anyway. Carmen slipped through his bedroom door. Closed it behind her. She swept her hand in front of her.

"Separate bedrooms, huh?"

He shrugged. Took a half step back. Froze in confusion. Like a squirrel staring at a car slowing down at an intersection.

She lowered her head. Looked up at him through the fall of red curls. Pulled off her tank top as she took a step deeper into the room. Rose up on her toes as she unbuttoned her shorts.

It didn't matter how he looked. Standing there naked in stark light in front of a stranger. And he had to admit that's what she was. And like him, her body had been lived in. Imperfect. Flawed and scarred — and he saw it as beautiful.

How had his failures earned this for him? What had he done that made him deserve a woman offering herself to him so freely? Without reservations or demand.

She walked into the bathroom. Her skin was so pale, every line and freckle seemed to shout at him. She dragged her nails through his chest hair as she passed to step into the shower. Took his hand to pull him in with her.

His body responded before his mind, and she looked up with a grin as the water saturated her hair. Flattened it down and trickled down the ridge of the scar in front of her ear.

She reached down and pushed his erection aside. Took his shoulder in her other hand to turn him around.

He smelled the soap before he felt her hands on his back. She started right in the center. That spot he could never quite reach.

Chapter Twenty-Two

FRANK STOOD in front of the stove. Pushed the bacon out of the way to make room for the egg he was about to crack into the grease. And paused to look behind him.

Carmen sat at the table. On the edge of the seat, kicking her feet so her toes dragged across the floor. Little whispers of sound. Like a mouse's heartbeat.

She grinned at the sight of him looking. Tipped her head to the side so her damp hair fell down the side of her face. Waved at him before turning to look out the window.

Frank went back to making the breakfast he'd promised her. Hissing when the bacon popped a bit of burning grease onto his chest.

She had put her complete outfit back on. Frank had stopped at the shorts. A long cargo style with ties at the knees.

They had stayed in the shower until the water started to cool. Alternating between washing and rinsing. Each doing their own part. Like doing the dishes.

Frank laughed to himself at that thought. Something so

mundane to describe what they had just done. And looking back into his memory — savoring a few of the moments with his eyes closed while the bacon sizzled — and he was *sure* she was playing him.

Carmen was twenty years older than the girls from the cookout yesterday, and he was twenty years older than her. There was no way she had fallen for him in a few days. Impossible to imagine she felt anything for him except what she thought she could maybe get.

Revenge against an abusive partner? Some forbidden love? Something more? Something *worse*?

He still couldn't keep himself from living in this moment. The feeling of a woman behind him while he cooked them breakfast. Something so … *domestic*.

The sex was amazing. Even with Sarah, he'd had no complaints. But even that much pleasure was just a need fulfilled. He mostly missed the presence of another person. And not a *Stan*, but a significant other. An emotional partner. Someone to share life with.

Frank was better when he was with somebody else. He could think clearly. Imagine and plan. Apply mental energy to more than the emptiness inside him.

He looked back at her again. Felt a twinge of regret cut through his joy. He knew it would be good while it lasted, but something was going on in Playa Dolor, and he knew she and Preston were a part of it. There was no doubt that this all would come to an abrupt and painful end, but Frank had no choice. He would do almost anything — *ignore* almost anything — just to feel this again.

He was happy to stay silent while he finished up, and she seemed to feel the same way. He imagined it was just another day. Like a hundred other mornings they had shared before.

He plated the food — over twice as much on his — and turned to find Carmen looking up at him with a half smile. Like she was proud of him. He waited for her to say something, but she only kept looking.

He brought the breakfast to the table. "Bacon, eggs over medium, and wheat toast with cinnamon butter. Your meal is served."

She leaned back. Clapped her hands as if applauding a play. Sarah had been a serious woman. He had never much gone for the cutesy childish nonsense that a lot of women perfected. The pouty lips and helpless routine.

Solid and confident. Sure of thought and action. Frank was attracted to *women*. Not girls. But seeing Carmen bounce in the chair with childlike excitement made him aware of how alluring something like that could be.

It made men feel powerful and dominant. A dangerous dynamic, in his opinion.

And Frank was sure many women didn't do it on purpose. To some women, it was a part of their behavior. Whether learned in childhood, or later during social experimentation with the discovery of boys, or affected in adulthood as a means to an end, it worked.

Fathers and daughters. That special bond. And Frank had to admit that whenever Jenny had looked up at him with her wide eyes and pouting demands, he had given in almost shamelessly.

But there were men that couldn't separate protection from exploitation. Sexualizing an ideal.

Animals.

He smiled at Carmen as she settled down and grabbed her fork. Tore a hole in the egg so the yolk ran. Dipped the corner of the toast into the yellow drizzle. Met his gaze as she put the bite into her mouth. Like a cooking show judge tasting a contestant's offering.

Frank looked at his plate. Dug in with gusto, only glancing back up at the sound of her laughing.

He raised his eyebrows in question, and she shook her head. "It's just you look so happy. Did I have something to do with that?"

"Am I not usually happy?" Frank asked instead of answering.

She sobered. Leaned forward to study his face. "No. You are usually very sad. I've seen you on the beach. Running like something's chasing you." Then she leaned back and tipped her head in thought. "Actually, no. You *don't* seem sad. You seem angry. Except for now."

"I don't seem angry now?"

She pulled in a slow breath through her nose. "No. Relaxed and happy. But distracted, too."

He wiped his mouth and leaned back to match her posture. Looking down his nose to inspect her across the table. "Distracted by what?"

"Hopefully me."

"You *want* to be a distraction?"

"To help you escape from whatever you're running from? Absolutely."

He looked away. Felt the blissful moment slipping through his fingers. He closed his eyes. Gritted his teeth against the anger he knew she could see. Forced it down so he wouldn't direct it at her.

His heart pounded. Heat rolled across the skin of his face. Down into his neck. *No …*

A panic attack at the breakfast table. Right in front of a woman he had been using to distract himself from the pain of his failure.

Shame gave Frank a roiling cramp in his guts, and he leaned forward to cover his face with his napkin.

Her chair made a squealing groan as she pushed it

back to stand. Bare feet slapping off the tile. And she took his head in her hands. Pressed his face into her belly and held him against her as he broke down.

He didn't know this woman. Wasn't sure of her motives. Lifted his hands to push her away. Clung to her instead.

She rubbed her hands from his scalp down the back of his neck. In a steady rhythm. A soothing cycle of sensation he could focus on instead of looking at what was causing him to weep into a stranger's skin.

It didn't matter that they'd had sex. What they had done to and for each other. It didn't matter that he was falling into some kind of obsession. She was still a stranger, and he was in trouble.

In spite of knowing the fight he was in for, Frank was losing. Carmen could ask him to do anything. Demand his every secret. And he knew he would do it.

He pulled her down into his lap. Apologized into her ear. Winced at the sound of his own voice. Horse and desperate. Shook his head at his behavior.

Apologized again.

She shushed and soothed. Rubbed his back. Whispered right back.

He had told Stan often enough. But *only* Stan. He knew if he said anything to her, she would have him. She would win. Before he even figured out the rules of the game.

"I miss her so much." Frank collapsed against her as the pain came flooding back.

Images of Jenny's body. Sarah begging him to stop looking for their daughter's killer. The accusation on the faces of the cops in Creek County. The feel of the gun in his hand when he shot Patrick Dahl. When he shot Malick Briar.

The way his satisfaction in their killings could never fill the emptiness.

"Who?" Carmen said.

"She was the best part of me."

Carmen didn't ask again. Just held him while he cried as their breakfast got cold.

Chapter Twenty-Three

FRANK HAD MANAGED to regain control. Pushed Carmen off his lap. Escaped out the back door only to find her rushing to catch up.

He tried fending off her efforts to comfort him, but her hand fit inside his so well. The ground he had reclaimed slipped from his grasp, and he was lost again. Crying against her, cursing himself for wasting time for them both.

For the hundredth time, Frank wondered how he got there. Had Stan lured him, or had he lured Stan? Or were they both holding each other back?

The memory of Sarah at his side was now tempered by the feel of Carmen in his arms. The image of Jenny's face sinking deeper into the depths of the flood he felt all around him.

He tried to pull away, but Carmen hung on. Followed him as he stumbled into the sunshine. Over the sharp dunes and down toward the water.

She steered him away from the surf, and like a small child throwing a fit in his mother's arms, Frank pulled his feet out from under him and plopped down into the sand.

Bore down on the pressure inside him and refused to shed another tear.

He refused to spare another moment feeling sorry for himself.

Carmen slid down next to him, his resolve solidifying into a promise at the sight of her fading bruise. A vow to stop making excuses. Like the hardened center of a burned log. A core of strength while everything around it flaked away.

She allowed herself to be pulled into him. Sat in the silence he needed. Until the sweat rolling down his face hid the tracks of his tears.

He sat up like coming out of a dream. "I'm so sorry."

She put her hand flat on his chest. "For what?"

He waved at the beach, like the answer was there for her to see. "For just … pulling you into my nonsense. Sweating all over you. I'm just … I'm sorry."

She laughed. Like cool water poured over his head. "Don't worry about me. I *love* this kind of heat. The hotter the better. Sticky humidity. A steamy breeze."

She pulled her shirt from her skin. A streak of moisture made it cling to her breasts. "An excuse to wear less clothing. Of course, I have to slather myself with two thousand SPF, but we all pay for the things we love, don't we?"

He thought of Stan's guilt. His own shame. Nodded to himself. The things a person thought about the most was what that person truly loved. Or at least what was most important to them, whether they meant it to be or not.

He pointed to her injured eye. "Like that?"

Her forehead wrinkled in confusion, and she reached up to touch her cheek at the edge of the discolored skin. Then she smiled in sudden understanding. "Some payment is more than others. Some we're willing to pay … maybe not *happily*, but willingly, yeah."

"And others?"

Carmen shrugged. Put her hand back on his chest. "You tell me. What's too high a price for you?"

He pushed her hand away. Cast a look over her shoulder. "I haven't found what I'm unwilling to pay yet. So I keep raising the price."

Carmen followed his gaze, then whipped her head back around. "What are you looking at?"

"Do you think Preston would be angry seeing us sitting here together like this?"

"Like what? One neighbor helping another through a crisis?"

"Is that what you call what we did in the shower?"

She grinned. Squinted up at him. "Did it make you feel better?"

Frank looked away as he nodded. "Oh yes. Much."

She brushed her fingers over his chest. Down his belly. Then she slid her hand into his waistband. "I can make you feel better again."

He grabbed her wrist. Pulled her hand away, and the frustration on her face made him laugh. "No."

"Why not?" Her voice rose into a whine, and Frank realized she was genuinely angry that he had stopped her.

"Because I don't want you to feel like you *have* to do that."

She frowned and pulled her hand from his fingers. "You didn't … you don't …"

She trailed away, then Frank took her hand and returned it to his chest. "Carmen, I was recently told something that I'm going to now say to you. If you only felt about yourself the way I feel about you, you would see that I want *this*. Just this. Being with you. Being accepted by you. While the sex was incredible — and more than I deserve — this is what I want. To *be* with you. This moment. Right now."

She narrowed her eyes, and tears glistened on her cheeks. "I don't understand."

He slid back to get enough room to face her. "Has nobody ever said that to you?"

"That they just want me? That I'm worth more than a quick fuck in the bushes?" Carmen shook her head. "No."

He was shocked by how sad that made him. For a moment, Frank wondered what it would have been like to meet Carmen before her opinion of herself had been shoved to the floor. Well before it would have been appropriate or even *legal* for him to know her, probably.

At his age, it probably wasn't appropriate to know her *now*. "I'm sorry that your life has led you to believe what you've been told."

Her mouth fell open. "Jesus, I believe you."

"I hope so."

"No, I mean I believe you are *really* sorry. You give enough of a shit about a person trying to … a person you don't even know … I don't understand you. Do they even make men like you anymore?"

"I'm sure they do."

"Well I haven't met him yet. Or at least, not until you."

Frank shook his head. "I'm not special. I can just tell when somebody else is."

Carmen pushed herself away. Jumped up to put her hands on her hips. "Like *that*. How do you *do* that? Ever since the frat party in the parking lot yesterday, I've done nothing but think about you. *Dreamed* about you. I'm obsessed — like a teenager — and it makes me sad that you'll be going soon."

Frank shielded his eyes and stared into her gaze as he

stood. His sudden suspicion made his mouth feel like the sand underfoot. "What makes you think I'm leaving?"

"Because that's what always happens." She dropped her head with a whisper. Barely a sound over the warm wind.

"What always happens?"

Carmen shrugged. "They leave. The good ones never want someone like me."

His suspicion surrendered to sympathy, and he stepped into her. This time, she cried into *his* chest. He bent his neck forward. Pushed his lips into her hair. "I can't stop thinking about you either."

"*But?*"

"But what?"

"There's always a *but*."

He sighed. "I guess you're right. I have to leave."

She nodded. "I knew it."

"But not because of you."

"Sure."

"Carmen, please."

"Sure." She twisted out of his embrace. Wiped her face. "You mind walking your neighbor home?"

He looked down the beach again. "What about Preston?"

She sneered. "He won't be back until late tonight. I'm lonely."

She held her hand out, and he took it. Let her pull him into a slow walk. All the way to the door of her enclosed porch where they stood in the shade of a metal eave.

A fan hummed in the corner. Oscillating to blow warm air through the dark screen. Frank could make out the stack of wine boxes. The shape of her easel, with a pile of blankets in front of it. Empty wine glass. A scatter of prescription bottles that made him wince away with the memory of what too many pills could do to a woman at war with her emotions.

Carmen stood on her tiptoes and breathed into his face. Draped her arms on his shoulders. "I'm sure you loved your daughter very much."

He clenched his teeth. Nodded as he looked away. She shouldn't even know such a thing, let alone say it out loud.

She pulled against the back of his neck. "And I'm sure she knew it."

He thought about Jenny's smile. The birthday card she had made out of shoebox cardboard. *I LOVE YOU GREAT BIG BUNCHES* written in sprawling letters across the inside. Decorated with unicorn stickers.

"I think she did," he agreed.

"It doesn't matter what *you* think. I know you're a good man."

Carmen didn't know he was lying to her. Using her. Or maybe she did. But she couldn't know he was a killer.

"And you are more than the pleasure you can provide. So much more."

She smiled. "Maybe. But right now that's all I want to be."

She reached behind her to open the door. Pulled him into the heat. Frank gave her some playful resistance, but followed her inside. Eased the door shut behind him.

"You seem to be an independent woman. Who am I to argue?"

This time when her hand slipped behind his waistband, Frank didn't stop her.

Chapter Twenty-Four

FRANK SAT with his back in the corner. The rough screen scratching against either shoulder. Carmen sat between his splayed legs. Leaning back on his chest.

She poured a fresh glass of wine for each of them. Passed his back over her shoulder.

The fan rotated with a creak of plastic. Blew warm air across his exposed skin that did little to cool him off. The sweat between their bodies trickled down like crawling ants.

Carmen was free with her image. Much more than Sarah had ever been. He wasn't sure if it was a lack of self-consciousness, or just that she had been seen by too many eyes to care any longer. Sarah had always wanted the lights off while undressing.

She had been free with the *touch* of her body, just not the appearance.

Frank had never been ashamed of the things he couldn't control. Moles, scars, and birthmarks. His old paunch had bothered him. His growing love handles. As he had proven, he'd been able to correct those issues, but for a long time, he had been ashamed of his body. Or rather, how his body illustrated his lack of care.

He hadn't minded Sarah turning the lights off, because then she couldn't see how he was letting his own body go.

He wished she could see him now, then he flushed with shame. How selfish and self-centered could he be? He gulped the wine. Tipped his head back into the corner.

They talked through a matching set of bottles. Nothing of consequence. Like strangers staying away from the serious topics. The shadows of each other's lives hanging over them.

He curled forward. Hooked his arm around her waist. Hung his beard over her shoulder to rest his head against hers. The sound of her hair rubbing against his ear was like static.

This was coming to an end. For all of his recent sins, the immorality of being with her was weighing on him. One way or the other, it had to stop.

The lying. Especially the lies he told himself. But until then … Frank slid his hands over the slick of her skin. Found the sensation in the moment. Waited for her to find it too.

She giggled when his stomach rumbled, then hopped up to dance away. He watched her disappear into the kitchen. Gasped as the wash of cool air from inside rolled across him.

She came back holding a small container of blueberries and a box of Triscuits. She sat down cross-legged in front of him. Shivered as she put the fruit down to open the crackers. Frank could see the goosebumps all over her arms and shoulders.

He wondered what Stan was doing. Then Carmen

handed him a cracker with a blueberry on it, and by the time they were done with the adult version of a Lunchables, the berries were gone, and a third bottle was empty, and they were in each other's arms again.

Frank knew what was waiting for him. Facing his mistakes was like staring into Jenny's eyes while she demanded to know why he had failed to deliver on his promise.

It made him desperate to get as much from Carmen as he possibly could. To give as much as she asked for. And the end drew nearer and nearer.

He could tell she felt it too. In her hesitance to let go. How she clung to him. And how he held her back. Frank could only imagine the life she was returning to. The one she obviously didn't want.

He thought of Preston holding her arm in anger. The black eye she seemed to be lying about. Perhaps it wasn't as hard to imagine as he had first thought. How many women lived like that? In constant fear and pain.

Abused until they could no longer even understand their value.

He choked back tears. And when Carmen dug her fingertips into his shoulder blades, Frank knew she had heard him. He barely finished before he started crying again.

He couldn't count the number of times he'd lost control lately. Breaking down and weeping out of nowhere. He rolled off of Carmen with a hissing wince. Threw his forearm up to cover his eyes. "I'm sorry."

Her hand on his thigh like fire. "No. It's fine. I understand."

She pushed up onto her knees. "It's been far more than I expected. More than I hoped. Oh!" Carmen sat back on her heels and put her hand over her mouth. "That sounded terrible. That's not—"

Frank dropped his hand and laughed. Shook his head as more tears squeezed through his eyelids. He caught his breath and sighed. "I know what you meant, but I think I did pretty good for an old man."

Carmen stood with a soft grunt. "You did good for *any* man. I'll be right back."

He braced himself for the blast of cold air. Winced as it kissed his sweat. Groaned when his head began to throb.

Should have been drinking water instead of wine. How many bottles had they gone through? He'd been here for hours. Should have had something more substantial than crackers and berries.

Frank propped himself up on his elbows. Closed his eyes against the way the room seemed to tilt in his vision.

Carmen came back out carrying a wet washcloth and a towel. Stooped down next to him, and he pushed her away, shaking his head, but she still brought the washcloth down.

He tried to grab it away from her, but she slapped his hand. Her face held the same determination he remembered from when she had thrown her leg over him on the end of the pier. Carmen wasn't having it.

He didn't like the feeling of being serviced. Plus, she was rather rough. Then he wondered why she hadn't invited him to clean himself up inside.

What was she hiding?

She finished to roll the washcloth and towel into a tight bundle she threw to the side, and Frank was suddenly aware of the pressure in his bladder.

Carmen leaned to the other side to scoop her shirt off the floor. Struggled to pull it down over her sweaty shoulders. Her hair popped through like an opening flower, and she grinned as she worked the bottom down.

He grinned back. Got to his knees to reach for his shorts and underwear. Noticed a hole in the seam of the boxers. Snorted laughter as he stood to pull them on.

On his feet, the pain in his head rose to a pounding. He rubbed his temples. Turned to find her looking up at him. His hands fell to hang limp at his side. His shoulder sagged. "I want to say something to you, but I don't know what it is."

She wrapped the front of her shirt around her fists. Pushed them down between her legs. Looked at the floor. "I know what I want it to be."

"What?"

"The same thing *every* girl wants to hear, I guess." Her words were slurred, swaying as she rose to her knees. "But I know you can't."

"How do you know?"

"Because it would be a lie, and I know you would never be dishonest with me."

Her words were an icy counterpoint to his boiling headache. An accusation she had made without knowing how damaging it really was. He wanted to drop down on all fours. Take her head in his hands and tell her everything.

He wanted to tell her how he was forgetting his wife and daughter. Forcing his old life away so it could no longer hurt him. He wanted her to know that it had been easier thanks to her.

Frank even wanted to tell her that he was falling in love, but he couldn't. And not because it would be a lie. To his sickening regret, he no longer had trouble lying. No, his silence proved him a coward.

Before he could figure out what to say, she dropped back down and looked at the blanket under her shins. "Goodbye, Wendall."

He nodded. Swallowed the lump burning in the back of his throat. "Goodbye, Carmen."

The screen door shut behind him, and Frank somehow knew he would never see her again. If she started to cry, he hoped to God she waited until he was too far away to hear it.

Chapter Twenty-Five

HIS HEAD POUNDED with vigor every time he concentrated on his confusion. Like the mental energy made his heart pump harder but not faster. The pain subsided when he focused on the physical.

He was tired and hungry. An emptiness that reached into every corner of his body. And for the first time in his life, Frank knew why he felt that way. A simple need. To love, not to *be* loved.

But everyone he loved suffered.

He walked back up the boardwalk with his head down, as if pulling a load behind him.

The Spark was in its spot, and he smelled grill smoke before seeing the plume drift up. Of course Stan was cooking. The world could be burning down around him, and he'd still be looking for a snack.

He and his cousin met at the back door. Stan held a platter piled with chicken and steak. Frank could smell the Cajun rub as he squeezed past. "You look like shit."

"Back at ya," Frank replied, but his heart wasn't in it.

He went straight to the fridge for a bottle of water and guzzled the whole thing down. Then two aspirin and another bottle before shuffling back to his bedroom to wash his face. He put a shirt on before joining Stan by the grill.

"Do we ever talk anywhere but over food?"

Stan shrugged. "Food is life. It makes sense."

"Where you been?"

Stan grinned. Reached behind him for the sweating pint glass on the deck railing. "You first."

Frank told him. Every detail he thought Stan needed to know. His beer was gone, and the meat was done by the time he finished.

Stan waved flies away from the platter. Said nothing as he picked it up and went inside. Frank followed him. Sighed with relief as he sat at the kitchen table. Leaned back to enjoy the cool air inside.

"Mo's got a friend who works for a cellular phone company outside of Tampa."

Frank cracked one eye open. "Is that right?"

Stan slid a plate across the table. A huge steak with a layer of salt and pepper on it. Fork and knife on a folded paper towel. Frank had to swallow before the burst of saliva could work through his lips.

Stan nodded as he opened two Coronas. "Yup. They use the same towers that Top Mobile uses. He was able to get a log of the calls coming to our old phones."

Frank held his breath as he chewed the first bite. Had trouble paying attention to the details. "Okay?"

Stan paused to take a huge bite of his own before answering. "Just a snapshot of who's been trying to call us, you know?"

Frank closed his eyes. "Who?"

"Lots of spam, mostly. But one number kept coming

up. Your little beach friend from Heirloom Cove. Freya Dahl."

Frank looked out the window. "She's better off."

"Yeah, but you ain't. Hearing her voice might do you good. And she's probably worried sick about the nice old man that stopped calling her out of the blue. If she got news of the house burning down, she probably thought you were dead. Until the cops showed up, anyway."

"It's dangerous for her."

Stan sighed in frustration. "You been running around here with your dick at half-mast for days. If the chick you're boffing ain't playing you, then do you think she might be in danger if Owens catches up to us?"

"Nobody knows we're here."

Stan spread his hands. "I ain't the one been talking to the neighbors. Or whatever you been doing."

Frank focused on his steak. Cutting small bites. Forking them in and chewing methodically. "She said he was coming home tonight."

"So?"

"I just want to watch."

"Watch what, Frank?"

"What is that supposed to mean?"

Stan threw his head back and shook his head at the ceiling. "It means what it sounds like."

Frank saw Carmen's face. The bruise around her eye. The finger marks dug into her arm. Preston's anger. He shrugged. Stabbed another bite of steak.

"Wait a minute," Stan said. "What are you watching for exactly?"

"I want to see if he comes back in the boats."

"With more of those bags?"

"That's right."

"That's fucking bullshit is what that is."

Frank let his fork clatter to the plate. "What do you want from me?"

"How about the fucking truth. This is no way to treat your husband."

Frank snorted laughter. Covered his lips so he didn't spit out his half-chewed mouthful.

Stan put his hands over his heart. "And after I slaved over that hot grill for your dinner."

Frank managed to swallow. Washed it down with the rest of his beer. Leaned back to catch his breath. "Okay. Fine."

Stan grinned. "Then let's have it."

Frank crossed his arms. Thought it might make him look too guarded. Dropped his hands in his lap. Became afraid it made him look too passive.

"Oh, for fuck's sake! Just spit it out already."

"I want to ask her to come with me."

Stan froze. "What are you, in high school? Like you're going away for the summer and your childhood sweetheart has to stay in band camp or something? Are you fucking kidding me?"

Frank set his jaw. "No, I'm not. I'm going to have a conversation with Preston. Make sure he's aware of how we feel for each other. Then I'll ask her to come with me."

Stan stared for a moment before jumping up and marching to the fridge, where he pulled out the rest of the six pack, then stomped back to his chair with a growl. "First off, you don't know where we're going. Second, I doubt you really mean to *talk*. Third, I don't have a *third* because this is too fucking insane."

He slid a fresh beer across the table.

Frank grabbed the bottle and pressed the cool glass to his forehead. "It's what I want. It doesn't even really matter if she comes. I just need to ask."

"Do you really think you can save her? And for that matter, does she even *need* saving? She's probably only the third chick you ever laid."

"Certainly not," Frank said.

Not *many* more than three, though.

"So how you wanna do it?"

Frank was confused by Stan's sudden change. Amenable to a plan he clearly didn't agree with. "Like I did before, I guess."

"Watch the ocean from Barney's bedroom? Maybe get a little action while we wait?"

Frank smiled. "I do owe you for dinner."

Stan tipped the bottle up. Wiped his lips. "Let's say he comes back with another load."

"I wanna find out what it is."

"For leverage?"

"Yes."

"Then have your talk?"

"Yes."

"Then ask your new girlfriend to run away with you?"

"That's right."

"Do you know how batshit crazy this is?"

Frank finished his second beer. Reached his open hand across the table for a third. "I do."

"Why?" Stan filled Frank's hand with another Corona. "Why do you want this so much?"

Frank saluted with the bottle before taking a drink. "She deserves somebody on her side."

"But a stranger?"

"Just somebody."

"Pussy was that good?"

Frank drew back. Offended and angry. Stan held up both hands. "Look, I'm sorry. Just tell me why, okay?"

Frank sighed. "I don't think she'll come with me. I

think she's stuck. Probably feels like nobody cares about her. Taking pills. Probably too many by the looks of the bottle I saw on the floor. She definitely drinks too much."

Stan chuckled. "You *would* know about that one, wouldn't you?"

Frank pointed to Stan's bottle. "And what's that you keep putting in your mouth?"

"This? It's medicinal."

"Uh huh. Anyway. it wasn't the sex, but the words. The few we shared, anyway."

"I can imagine what *you* said. You're a hopeless romantic. Smoother than a bottle of lube. The ladies always fawned all over you."

"Really? I never noticed."

"That's why they did it. Shit drives 'em wild."

Frank felt uncomfortable imagining himself that way. Desirable? Just because he was *nice*? "She was just ... she said good things about me. Made me feel better about some of the things I've done."

"Like what?"

"I've done a lot of terrible things. Where do I start?"

"No numb-nuts," Stan shouted. "What did she *say*?"

"Oh." Frank wasn't sure he wanted Stan to know every detail. But the one thing that hit him hardest sprang to mind. "She said she knew I had been a good father."

Stan sat forward. Put his beer down so hard, it roiled up in a chimney of foam to rain over his knuckles. "She said that exactly?"

Frank started to nod. Then thought back. "No, she said she was sure I loved my daughter very much. Said she was sure Jenny knew it."

Stan slung beer from his hand. Leaned forward until his ribs hit the edge of the table. "You told her about Jenny?"

"What? No!"

"Then how did she know you had a fucking daughter? That you *had* a daughter?"

Frank's mind went back to the closed laptop. Then to the first time he had sex with Carmen. She had said Preston wanted her to do something. Something she didn't want to do. Something he had punished her for refusing.

It was him. Frank was sure of it. Preston had asked her to fuck some information out of him. She had refused. Probably because he was an old man. A stupid, stupid old man.

The marks on her arm. Preston hurt her, so she did what he asked. And Frank had let enough slip for her to figure out who he was.

He dropped his head into his hands.

"Welp," Stan said, "after we pack, we'll wait for Preston to get home. Have a chat to see what's up. Convince him and his old lady to keep their mouths shut. Or we'll shut 'em ourselves. Goddammit, Frank. Tell me tomorrow if she was worth it."

Stan pushed away from the table and walked away.

But Frank didn't have to wait; he knew the answer already.

Chapter Twenty-Six

THE NEXT FEW hours were spent in tense silence. Frank in his part of the house. Stan in his.

Frank looked down at everything he had arranged on his bed. Like he was getting ready for the school dance. Dark pants. Dark T-shirt. A black neck gaiter to hide his snowy beard. Black beanie. Boots. Comfortable socks.

A multi-tool in a canvas pouch. Dark belt with five ammo loops. Each one holding a magazine of .380 rounds. His pistol sitting next to the holster that clipped to his waistband. Small flashlight. Binoculars on a leather strap.

Frank dressed like the act was a ritual. Each step full of care and attention. Pausing for a moment to marvel at the ease of tying his laces. Not too long ago, he had begun to change his mind about slip-on shoes to avoid the effort of reaching past his expanding gut, but now ... self-abuse seemed to be doing the trick.

He stood to finish his preparation by sliding on his belt. Adjusting the pouches and loops. Glanced up at the imposter in the mirror.

Killed his bedroom light as he left, and it felt like the last time he'd ever turn it off.

Stan was at the kitchen table. Instead of food spread out in front of him, it was guns. Two .45's. A pair of dark green canteens nestled in matching pouches sat on the edge under the window.

Stan didn't look up when Frank came in.

Frank slid the chair out. Dropped into it, careful to keep from jostling the table.

Stan pointed to the far canteen. "That one's yours."

Frank pulled it over. "What are we in for?"

Stan shrugged. "You tell me."

Frank sighed as he clipped the canteen to his belt. "We wait and we watch. Then we take care of business."

Stan holstered one pistol. Then the other. "Do you even know what that business *is*?"

"I think so."

Stan shook his head. "I'm as much to blame as you, Frank. I haven't been doing right. By you or by me. You need help I can't give. I saw it a long time ago, but I just let it build. Until here we are. But it may not have to get ugly. Like you said. We'll watch."

Frank looked out the window. "It's about to be full dark. How about it?"

Stan pushed to his feet. "Lemme get a quick bite first. Something light."

Frank watched his reflection pass behind him. Cross to the cabinet next to the fridge. Stan pulled down a box of Honey Buns. Leaned against the counter and ate two in a row.

He brushed both hands on the front of his shirt. "Okay. Now I'm ready."

Frank spun in the chair. Stood without comment.

Turned the lights off and let his eyes adjust to the darkness in the rear of the hall.

He held his breath as he emerged into the heat of the evening. Walked in front of the Spark. To the dry grass on the other side of the gravel driveway. He stopped behind a willow tree. Ducked under the drooping limbs and settled before taking a deep breath.

A smell he would forever associate with murder. Not death. Natural. Unavoidable. But *murder*.

Like when he had killed Briar to let his body sink into a marsh very much like this one. Only it didn't have the toxic algae. Or the painful cuts on the bottoms of his feet.

Or Carmen.

Frank sighed as Stan ducked into the shadow beside him. He leaned toward his cousin and whispered, *"We can go from tree to tree for a while, but the last several yards are wide open from the road to the waterway."*

He could see Stan's nod of understanding, so he turned to head down the lane. Keeping an eye in both directions for lights. Cocking his ear up for sounds other than the soft scrape of their own boots.

By the time they had made their way to the thinning cover, darkness had deepened into a clinging black among the trees. Frank paused for a moment. Straining for the sound of somebody coming down the road. Or through the water. Squinting into the distance, looking for lights or movement.

Finally, Frank dropped into a crouch and rushed into the open. To the edge of the bridge railing where he fell to his knees and waited for Stan to follow. His cousin's feet were quiet as he ran, but his breath was harsh and gasping.

With Stan in position, Frank rolled around the edge of the rail. Straight to Barney's back door, where he eased it open, ducked inside, then held the door open for Stan to follow.

When they were both situated inside, Frank closed the door. Threw the deadbolt before standing with a sigh of relief. "We are dramatic idiots."

Stan was a lump in the dark kitchen. "Maybe. But you either fail to prepare or prepare to fail."

Frank snorted. "Does that really apply to this situation?"

"You rather walk down the center of the lane naked?"

"No, it just seems like we're missing a middle ground."

Stan pressed past him toward the rear of the house. "Like I said … maybe. But this is way more fun, isn't it?"

Frank didn't want to admit that Stan was right, but it *was* fun. Doing something with a purpose — no matter how useless that purpose turned out to be — was always more satisfying than doing something just because. Activity without results was a drag.

Frank cupped the end of the flashlight in his palm before turning it on. A gentle red glow of light bled through his skin, enough to turn the featureless shapes into couches and chairs and coffee tables.

He led Stan though the obstacle course. Into Barney and Melody's bedroom. He paced into the space between the bed and the window. Clicked off the flashlight as he sat down.

Stan plopped right next to him. Raised his own binoculars. Keyed the night vision on to bathe his face in a subtle wash of green. Pressed through the gap in the curtains. "Where am I looking?"

"Their pier is pretty much straight ahead. The house is way right."

Frank dropped to his knees to put his binoculars under the curtain. He regretted wearing the beanie. Sweat was dripping down his neck. Crawling down his back. Along his ribs.

He wanted to scratch at every drop.

He started with the house. Steadied on the glass.

Lights in the screened-in porch were on. Carmen stood with her arms crossed in the center of the room. A bottle of wine hanging from her right hand.

Her hair bounced like she was shaking her head. Frank was convinced he would know the woman anywhere. Just from her silhouette.

"There's an empty boat tied at the end," Stan said.

Frank rotated left. "Did we miss something? Did they show up already?"

"They who?"

Frank turned back to the porch. Carmen had moved while he'd been looking away. She held the bottle out away from her. The other hand was up at the side of her head. On the phone?

She lowered the phone. Stood with her head down. Then she tipped her head back, and Frank imagined the sound of her scream.

She threw the phone into one corner. The bottle into another. Dropped to her knees.

Frank pulled away from the binoculars. Closed his eyes and pressed his forehead to the rubber rings around the eyepieces.

"We got lights on the water."

Frank sighted back into the lenses. Tracked to the ocean where he saw the flicker, bouncing on the waves as a small boat approached the shore. "There it is. Just like last time."

He looked back at the porch in time to see Carmen stand up and pull on her shirt.

"Damn, son," Stan said.

Frank glanced over to see his binoculars pointed at the porch. Wondered what Carmen looked like through the more advanced glasses.

She changed into a dark outfit. Tucking her hair into a knit cap that made her head look like the tip of a black condom. She turned out the lights on the porch, and when Frank found her shadow stomping down the path to the beach, he could tell she was angry.

Had that been Preston on the phone? What did he say to her?

"The fuck is that?" Stan said.

Frank turned to see figures on the boat wrestling with more of those same black bags he'd seen the first time. Like the reeking bags in the garage.

He couldn't tell who the figures were. Even when Carmen got into their midst, Frank had trouble picking her out. There was frantic activity he couldn't decipher.

"They're moving," Stan said.

Frank held as still as he could. Then he saw it. Whatever was inside those bags was now moving. Struggling to be free.

Chapter Twenty-Seven

FRANK STUDIED the figures as they hefted the load up to the top of the steps. Onto the long pier leading back to the house. The front two were definitely Carmen and Preston. More details revealed by the dim glow of landscape lighting that lined the boardwalk.

She was at the rear, and whoever was in the bag was kicking for all they were worth. Carmen was having trouble maintaining her line behind Preston. Swaying and stumbling with the writhing movements of their victim.

"Back to the house," Stan said. "We got new players on the field."

"Who?" Frank said as he turned back up the beach. Four men standing in the shadows. Still and stiff. Like they didn't want to be there. They were too close to each other for Frank to make out any features. Height or weight. Bearing.

"I don't know," Stan said. "Maybe when they all get together there, they'll space out a little. Fucking backs are all to me. I can't see any faces. Military haircuts, though. Maybe even cops."

Frank traced back to Carmen and Preston as they headed to the rear, probably going to the garage. Close on their heels were the other two figures from the boat. He couldn't tell from here, but he was sure it was Tan Man and Red from the picnic.

Friends? Employees?

Frank cursed himself for handling everything so poorly. He was staring uphill and there was a fire behind him.

Preston popped out from behind the house. Carmen close behind him. Frank watched them walk up to the new players. Preston was animated and open, but Carmen appeared more reserved.

Tan and Red went back toward the pier. To get rid of the boats? For another load?

Frank looked away from the retreating pair, then back at the group in time to see Preston and Carmen in each other's face. Fingers pointing. Heads back in anger.

"Get 'em, girl," Stan said.

Preston slapped her with a left that blurred up from his hip. She rocked back and he stepped into her with a right-hand punch that dug into her gut. Folded her over his arm as her feet left the ground.

Frank saw a flash of skin at her ankles. Realized she was even barefoot for this.

He wasn't aware of standing and charging away until he felt Stan pull him back down with a bear hug. "Have you lost your fucking mind?"

He tensed. Made creaking fists that dug his nails into his palms.

"This kind of thing is what got you here in the first place. Jesus Christ, Frank. Can you keep it together for one goddamned second, please?"

He relaxed. Deep breaths through his nose. "I'm gonna kill him."

"How about just tuning him up a little. I can agree he deserves *that* at least. Let 's see what's in those bags first."

Frank nodded. Clenched his teeth as he leaned forward to grab the fallen binoculars. "Okay, okay. I was just—"

"Buddy. I know what you were just. I get it. Let's keep looking. Get all the facts, you know?"

Frank raised the glasses again. Leaned into the window. He found Carmen first. On the ground with her knees drawn up. Rolling from side to side while covering her belly.

Preston stood, conversing with two of the new players. The other two were gone.

"Fuck," Stan hissed. "Where'd they go, Frank?"

"I don't know."

"What about the other two?"

Frank twisted to look down the pier. Tan and Red struggled with a fresh bundle. It seemed less active than the previous loads, but heavier. "They're coming back with another one."

"They just fucking left her on the ground."

Frank looked back to see Carmen struggling to her knees. She leaned over, puked next to the boardwalk, then stood. Hunkered over with her arms hugged across her middle as she staggered down the near side of the house.

Frank dropped the binoculars. "She's coming here."

"*Here?*"

"Not *here* here. Here to me. To *our* house."

"How do you know that?"

"I just do. What else does she have?"

"*SHHHHHHHIT.*"

Stan rolled off the bed to move back out of the bedroom in a practiced crouch. Much smoother than Frank could manage. One pistol already drawn and ready.

The night vision goggles bounced off his chest.

Frank followed with less polish. Ended up with his back pressed into the wall next to the back door.

"You good?" Stan whispered.

Frank took a deep breath. Reached behind him for his pistol. Slipped it out of the holster. Brought it around and racked the slide. Thumbed the safety off. Held it up in front of him with his finger lying against the trigger guard.

It felt like the first time he had smiled in days. He gave an exaggerated nod before turning to face the door.

Stan reached up and turned the knob with the fingertips of his left hand. Pulled the door open with a slight hiss of air. Moved with the swing to stay behind it.

The music of bugs and frogs was distracting chaos.

Frank saw nothing in the backyard. No passing traffic. He crept around the edge of the doorway to put his back to the house while Stan followed, getting to his knees on the other side of the rear deck. An almost mirror image of the one on the back of their house.

They traveled closer to the road in fits and starts. From position to position. Pausing to look and listen. Broad gestures and pointing.

At the bridge before crossing over, Frank froze at the sound of footsteps on gravel. Huffing breath. He rose to look over the railing to see Carmen.

Crying. Stumbling down the lane. Coming for him just like he said.

He barely got two steps down the bridge before Stan wrapped him up and pulled him down. He felt his cousin's lips pressed against his ear. Felt the heat of his hissing breath.

"Don't! Look through the trees at the fucking house."

Frank sprawled across the bridge to get his head into the space between the top and middle rail. Looked into an orange glow growing in the distance.

They were burning his house down again.

He dropped back on his ass. Turned to stare at where Stan's face was. Just a lightening of shadows next to him. "*I can't,*" he whispered.

Stan touched his shoulder. "You have to."

Carmen shouted. A wordless cry that brought Frank skidding to the other side to look over the railing at the lane where she stood pulling her sleeve out of Red's grip.

The shout had been indignation rather than pain, but that was little comfort when Red looped his fist over her arm to punch her face.

She fell to her knees. Her fingers dug into Red's shirt to keep her from falling over. He dug *his* fingers into her hair. Heaved her back to her feet.

Her strangled cry trapped Frank's breath in his throat. He was back on his feet. Sighting his pistol at Red's face. His finger tightening on the trigger.

"Get the fuck outta here!" A panicked voice from the trees on his right.

Stan pulled Frank down by the back of his waistband as two figures dashed toward them.

Frank's teeth clamped on the tip of his tongue as his butt pounded the planks. Blood filled his mouth, and he leaned aside to let it dribble from his lips.

The pressure of the explosion hit his chest before he heard it. A rocketing stream of color into the sky.

Carmen screamed, and another voice kept repeating an apology.

"I fucked up, man. I didn't mean it. Oh shit, I fucked up."

Stan crawled to the end of the bridge. Looked both ways like he was getting ready to cross a busy street. Reached back behind him and grabbed Frank by his collar.

Then he was dragged, back into the lane where they hugged the tree line on their way home.

The Spark looked like a giant popcorn kernel. Split open and burning.

"Man, I had five gallons of gas in the back," Stan said.

Frank shielded his eyes from the heat. "What for?"

"For fucking emergencies. They must have hit it with a Molotov cocktail or something."

"Five gallons of gas did this?"

"I mean, not by itself. It was probably the breaching charges."

"Damn it!"

Stan threw his hands in the air. "Is that the best you can do?"

Frank grabbed his cousin's sleeve. Pulled him close. "How about this? The fucking fire department is probably on their fucking way right fucking now. How about we get our asses down the fucking road?"

Stan pulled Frank into an embrace that put their foreheads together. "That ain't bad, old man."

They jogged back into the trees. Hit a steady pace until they hit the opening at Barney's. Frank turned it up after that. He didn't care if Stan could keep up or not.

Chapter Twenty-Eight

FRANK FORCED HIS BREATH DOWN. Through his nose. Slow and deep. Blowing it out through his open mouth to keep from gasping noisily.

He was still amazed at how quietly Stan was moving behind him.

He dropped low to the ground. Crawled a few feet down the slope toward the water. Angled toward the bridge that crossed the water to Carmen's.

Voices at the house tried to distract him from the splashing putter of a trolling motor coming their way. He stopped in the deep shadow under the end of the bridge. Saw the front of the little boat he remembered Tan Man steering through the thick algae. Sure enough, the front was followed by the slick blond ponytail. And the glimmer of orange light reflecting from the barrel of the man's upraised pistol.

Frank tensed to lunge. Felt pressure pass his left shoulder as Stan shot into the dark.

Tan Man barely looked up before Stan's weight crashed on top of him.

There was a plastic thump and a rubber squeak, then Stan leaned back with Tan Man held before him in a vicious chokehold. His feet drummed on the bottom. Slid up and down like the man was trying to run into the water.

Stan grunted. Made a bridge out of his body to put more pressure on Tan Man's neck.

Frank grabbed the edge of the boat. Nearly tumbled into the water. Sneered in disgust when he planted his foot into several inches of foul water to steady himself.

Stan rolled over to release Tan Man into the water. Frank expected him to float, but instead he sank out of sight with barely a sound.

Frank jumped in next to Stan. Dropped down out of sight and hissed, "Did you just kill him?"

Stan grimaced as he sat up. "I hope so. The little fucker stabbed me."

"Where?"

"Here in the boat."

Frank bit down on the manic laughter trying to choke past his teeth. "No, I mean—"

"I know what you mean, doofus. He got me in the leg."

"With what?"

"This." Stan held up a small pocket knife. Like something somebody might use to clean their fingernails.

"My goodness," Frank whispered. "You think you'll live?"

"Ha-ha. Fuck that guy anyway."

"You had to kill him, though?"

"Bro, these people just blew up our car."

"You mean that roller-skate?"

Stan grabbed the tiller of the small trolling motor mounted to the boat's rear. Rolled the handle to get them moving into the water that ran down the side of the property. Moved them into a quick circle to get back under the bridge. Along the opposite side of the property toward the garage.

The door was up a few inches. Frank could hear voices inside. See feet going back and forth. Light spread across the gravel to glitter off the dark water.

Stan steered them along the edge of the light. Into the shadows along the bank. He whispered, *"Let's go,"* then jumped out of the moving boat without looking back to see if Frank was following.

Frank felt the boat push away from the shore. Rushed to follow only to end up knee deep in stinking marsh. Struggled to keep from flinging curses at Stan's back.

Voices in the garage fell silent. Then he saw the light turn off, leaving a negative shape burned into his eyes whenever he blinked. Shouldn't have been looking right at it.

Water squelched in his boots. Frank knew it was his imagination, but he felt the skin burn and itch. Like the neurotoxins were working their way inside already. Something that normally took years of exposure — all in a few moments.

Stan stopped at the small access door in front of the garage to peek around the corner.

Frank came up behind him, but didn't slow down in time. Ran into him as Stan pulled back.

He looked over his shoulder in exasperation, but Frank didn't bother apologizing. Stepped back to give him room. Stan tried the knob in the side door. It clicked open, and the smell Frank remembered rolled out in a swollen cloud.

Stan lowered himself as he swung the door in. Led around the edge with his pistol and motioned for Frank to follow.

He joined Stan in the gloom. Froze at the sound of movement in the depths.

Frank put his hand on the floor and it came away sticky and wet. He wondered if it was blood.

A shape loomed next to them. Closer, he saw it was the white van. Bringing in more, or taking it away?

Stan turned to go around the nose. Feeling the hood with his bare hand as he passed.

Frank moved down along the side of the van, finally coming to a stack of dark bags. Piled carelessly to fill the space like a dam before a flood.

The smell was so strong there. Bitter and piercing. He laid his hand on the top bag. Just a touch. Like a lover's teasing caress. It moved at the touch. A slow rise of breath.

Frank's heart pounded in his ears. A rush of blood to swell into all he could hear. He slid his hand down the length of the bag. Found the zipper.

"*Yo*," Stan whispered. A harsh noise that barely sliced through Frank's rising fear.

Frank slid the zipper open. All the way down to the other end of the bag. Pointed his pistol at the ceiling. Reached inside.

Hard ridges of flesh beneath his palm. Dry and warm. A snorting sigh of breath. It wasn't a little girl inside the bag. One Frank feared would be bruised and bloody, looking up at him with pleading eyes.

He found a monster instead. His mind screamed a warning right before it thrashed out of the bag. Uncoiling and rising up with a whip crack of motion.

Frank threw himself back with a shout. Rolled down the side of the van as the alligator fell down the back side of the stack of bags.

His pistol connected with the window. Glass shattered. A concussive noise that trailed into the musical tinkle of crumbling glass.

Raised voices from inside. Thumping feet.

Frank wanted to jump up on the van. His imagination showing him the gator's snout shooting out from under the frame to bite him off at the knees.

The kitchen door opened. Flooded the garage with blinding light. The doorway filled with shadow as Red stepped through. Raised his gun.

Frank lifted his own in response. Stopped when he saw blood dripping from his fingers. Must have cut it when the window shattered.

The sound of the gunshot slapped against his ears. Cracked and echoed off the walls and van.

The top of Red's head opened up in a spurting spray of blood that splashed up on the wall above the door. A spattering fan on the ceiling.

Red's gun fell from his fingers as he collapsed to the side.

Stan rose from his knees to move out of the light.

Frank heard the slither of the alligator's big body under the van. Attracted by the smell of blood? By the noise and movement?

Words couldn't form in his mouth. Just a warbling cry of warning as the gator jumped out from the darkness, just like his mind had imagined a hundred times since his fingers first brushed its hide.

Dinosaur teeth snapped shut on Stan's leg just above his ankle. His scream of pain became terror when he looked down to see what had him. A nightmare come true.

It thrashed back and forth, and Stan's leg broke with a wet snap. He went down, and the sound of his head cracking off the floor was almost as loud as his shin bones breaking.

Frank raised his pistol to track the gator as it began to pull Stan back under the van. He fired into its thick body. The muzzle flash freezing its motion with every shot fired.

He popped the magazine. Fished a fresh one from his belt loop. Scrabbled back to put distance between him and the gator.

No movement from under the van. And Stan's harsh breath was the only sound.

"There he is," said a voice from the doorway.

Frank expected to see Preston and his gloating smile. Instead, it was a short man with an impossibly thick chest. Arms like tree limbs sprouting from a barrel. Hair cut so close, Frank could see the scalp gleaming through.

Detective Owens stepped down to kick Stan's hand. The pistol slid across the floor like it was on a patch of ice. Owens kept his gaze fixed on Frank as he stepped over Stan's still body.

Reached behind him as he stooped down to look at Frank in the light shining over his shoulder.

Frank thought he was grabbing handcuffs, but instead, he pulled a yellow-handled taser from a Velcro holster. Leveled it at his neck. "Go ahead and drop that, please."

Frank looked down to see the .380 in one hand. The magazine in the other. He set them both aside. Looked back up to see Owens nodding.

"That's better," Owens said. Gave Frank a smile he found hard not to return. Then Owens pulled the trigger on the taser.

Barbs shot from the end. Buried in the skin of Frank's throat right above his collarbone. Burning pain coursed through him. A woman screamed. He thought it was Sarah, but she said somebody else's name.

After what felt like an hour of muscles tightening and bucking, the pain released him, and Frank fell straight back. His head smacked the floor. A hollow sound that resonated through his sinuses. His vision dimmed, and he turned his head to the side as vomit gurgled up into his mouth.

He coughed and gagged. Pulsing light behind his eyelids.

He heard a single — *NO!* — then agony crashed into his face. The metal rattle of the garage door behind him as his head bounced back.

Footsteps.

A cool touch on his burning cheek.

Sinking darkness.

Chapter Twenty-Nine

COLOR WASHED ACROSS HIS VISION. Blue and red and white. Screaming sirens in the distance dragging Frank out of his sinking spiral.

Opening his eyes would put him at the scene of Jenny's murder. His baby girl sinking in the mud. Or would it be Rory Day?

Sarah. Or Carmen. Maybe he would see his own body. Bruised and bloody. Sinking into the soft marsh.

Frank opened his eyes, but only the right one seemed to receive any light. Dazed and unsteady by pain, he drew a deep breath. Swallowed thick blood. Curled his lips in disgust at the taste inside his own mouth.

He was sitting up in the rear of the van. Leaning against the back of the driver's seat. The double doors were open, but instead of looking at the inside of the garage door, Frank saw a smooth stone wall covered in chalky white paint.

He lifted a few inches and looked back over his shoulder. Couldn't see out of that eye. Turned the other way.

Peered out the windshield to see the flashing lights of rescue vehicles shining through the trees.

Somebody had thrown him into the van and driven it down to the RV park. A sudden worry for the kids made him wheel around, then freeze with a hiss of pain as the throbbing in his head exploded from the sudden movement.

A wave of nausea made him curl over his thighs.

A voice groaned, and Frank wasn't sure if it was his until he opened his eyes to see Stan stirring beside him. Smears of blood under him. A soaked bandage wrapped around his right leg from the knee down.

"You're still alive?" Frank's voice sounded like the biting silica washing up on the dunes. Sharp and cutting.

Stan grunted. "You sound surprised."

"An alligator ate you."

"He didn't eat me. Just a nibble. Then he spit me out."

"Probably because you tasted like shit."

"Oh, I like the new Frank." Stan turned his head to look over through squinting eyelids, then shook his head. "On second thought, never mind."

"Do I look that bad?"

"As bad as I taste, apparently."

Voices and movement outside the van. Scuffling footsteps. Carmen appeared in the cargo door opening. One arm trailing behind her, with a hand on her wrist, holding her back.

Carmen jerked against it. "Let go!"

"My God," Owens said from the other side of the doors. "Just let her in. I'm sick of the constant bickering."

"Fine," Preston said. "All I want is my money anyway."

"You'll get it. Just as soon as we get what *we* want."

Preston let go so suddenly that Carmen fell back in a crunch of gravel.

A laugh from outside, but Frank couldn't tell who it was. He assigned it to Owens. One more reason to hate him.

Carmen stood with a sniff. Cradling her elbow in front of her. She struggled into the back of the van. Sobbed as she worked her way forward on all fours. Once close enough, she stopped in open-mouthed horror.

He must have looked dreadful.

Both of her eyes were now black. The skin was split over the bridge of her nose. An ugly bruise bloomed across her cheeks. Dried blood flaked in the corners of her mouth.

"Aren't we a sight," Frank said.

She shuffled next to him. Straddled his thighs to sit in his lap. Leaned forward into the light, and her face became a grotesque mask of color and grief. She reached up to touch his face. Paused with a moan. Brought her hands down to settle on his. "I'm sorry."

"For what?"

Stan snorted. "Give me a fucking break."

The van rocked as Owens threw his weight up into the back. "Well, now that you're both awake, let's get to this while my brothers and sisters are busy at the other end of the road."

Preston jumped up behind him. "Fuck yeah. Finally."

Owens threw an annoyed glance over his shoulder. Rolled his eyes before turning back and squatting down to balance on his toes, favoring each of them with a smile. "I have to admit, you two were extremely hard to find."

Carmen lowered her head, and her hair brushed across his face. Frank leaned away from the fuzzy tickle as she lowered herself to his chest. Wrapped her arms around him and whispered. "*I'm sorry.*"

Preston looked down at her and shook his head. "Shut up, you dumb bitch. You almost ruined it anyway."

"How you two ever found each other is a mystery," Frank said in disgust.

Preston drew back in confusion. "The fuck does that mean?" Then his face opened into understanding. A nodding laugh. "Oh, that's funny. She's my *sister*."

Stan barked laughter. "You *are* a dumbass."

"I'm sorry," Carmen said again.

Frank sighed. It made sense now. She had never once defined their relationship. He had assumed, and since Carmen was conning him, she let him believe what he wanted.

He agreed with Stan.

Owens held up both hands. "Can we, please? Every time one of Kirby's delusional followers calls in with a lead, I have to spend a week investigating. It's getting in the way of … my other interests."

Frank closed his eyes as the memory of Ty Kirby's *In Our Midst* played out. The smug assurance that he would find Jenny's killer with the help of his fans. The toll-free number and the web link to report sightings of the animals that had committed such heinous deeds. Right under their noses. Or in their midst.

Frank opened his eyes to see Stan shaking his head in disbelief, his face drawn and gray.

"Your *other* interests?" Stan said. "Raping little girls isn't a fucking *interest*."

"You're right." Owens grinned. "It's actually a calling. The interest is framing the fathers. It's usually easy."

Stan pushed himself higher to sit up straight. "I was wondering. It didn't make sense to be gunning after the Pedophile Junction so hard when you were doing essentially the same thing."

Owens shook his head. "It's *not* the same thing. At all. What they do is disgusting. Puerile and unmeasured. Sex for profit. Besides, they were never my target. Frank was."

"Why? He didn't deserve that."

"You're right. But sometimes, you run into a girl so sweet ... so *exquisite* ... you just have to throw caution to the wind."

Frank's remaining sight blurred as tears filled his eye. "*The winds,*" he whispered.

Owens moved in between them. Dropped a hand on his holstered pistol. "That's right. I wish there was more of a reason to give you, but there just isn't. West didn't rape and kill your daughter. It was *me*. Over days. And it was the best experience of my life. Might have even been my *last*, but something went wrong when I tried getting them to arrest you. Mallory Black, specifically. If not for her screeching about how guilty you were, there would have been more cops willing to believe. She robbed a lot of us in just the wrong way."

"That's it?" Stan said.

"I'm afraid so." Owens nodded. "I was just training West in the art. Using Frank as an example. Maybe we both got too ambitious."

Frank wanted to believe there was more to it. That there was a deeper meaning to his daughter's death. But like many survivors, he had to face a hard truth. Sometimes bad things happened.

Carmen shuddered. The heat between them was a humid layer of sweat. He wanted to push her away. Fling her from the van. Tear Preston's throat out.

Then he wanted to hurt Owens the worst.

And with one deep breath, his fire cooled. Jenny had died. For no more reason than fate had looked away. Now he was going to die. Killed by the same man.

It seemed fitting. Almost satisfying.

Carmen rocked her hips. Made enough room between them to work her hands into the space.

"So now, I just need to know who you told." Owens pointed to Stan's bandaged leg. "That thing will rot off *way* before I let you go."

Stan rolled his eyes like a teenager embarrassed by their parents. "Like I'm supposed to believe you're gonna let us go."

Owens laughed like they had shared a private joke. "I guess not."

He lifted his hand. Brought it down like a hammer to smash into Stan's broken leg. Stan threw his head back and howled. His voice cracked, and he curled forward to retch into his lap.

Owens wiped his fist off on his pant leg with a sneer of disgust. "Just tell me who else knows. I'll find that black mountain from the gym. Moses? And his girlfriend. Something about her, I gotta admit."

Frank tried to keep his attention on Owens, but Carmen's movements were growing more insistent. He wanted to push her off and demand some consideration for the situation.

He turned his head. Tipped it back to get a view of what she was doing. Saw both of her hands up under her shirt. The flash of metal as she pulled a gun free. Covered in a sticky sheen of blood. It looked like the one Red had dropped in the garage after Stan shot him in the face.

Frank looked back at Owens. Slid his fingers up to meet Carmen's. Nestled under her breasts where she slid the weapon into his hand.

Frank lowered the pistol to sit along the outside of his leg. Swallowed more rancid saliva before clearing his throat. "You might as well kill us, then. Neither one of us knows where they are. And we haven't told *anybody*."

Owens pulled his sidearm. Pointed at Carmen's back. "What about her? You ever say something to her? Whisper in her ear about your sweet little girl?"

Carmen looked back over her shoulder. "He didn't even tell me his real name."

"That's right." Preston laughed. "For a long time, we thought his fucking name was *Wendall*."

Carmen pushed off from Frank so hard, his air grunted out in a painful *WHOOSH*. She spun around and launched herself at her brother. His face was a shock of confusion. He started to lift his hands, but it was too late.

Her clawed slap hit him on his right cheek. Drove him to the side where trails of blood flicked from her fingernails to splatter lines across the metal.

He threw himself back with a shout. Got his knees back under him and shot to his feet, but the van wasn't tall enough and his head bashed into the underside of the roof.

His eyes fluttered closed as he collapsed.

Frank burst out laughing.

Carmen took a stooped step and kicked Preston in the balls. His body curled up and rolled to the side. Carmen drew back for another, but Owens turned to hook her around the waist, then slung her back into the space between Stan and Frank.

She landed in a protective ball. Wept into her hands.

"This is ridiculous," Owens said.

Footsteps outside the van, and two of the men that had accompanied Owens stood in the opening. Neither looked particularly interested in what was happening inside.

The fourth man was probably in the car, or down talking to the cops at the end of the lane.

And where were all the kids?

Frank lost his train of thought when looking at Stan. His cousin's hand was inside the cargo pocket on the side of his leg. His gaze flinched up to meet Frank's eyes, then fell back to the floor under Owens.

Owens got up on one knee. Aimed his pistol at the ceiling. Sighed dramatically.

He opened his mouth to speak again, but he was interrupted by Preston's moan. When he glanced over in frustration, Stan whipped his hand up from his pocket. The flash of the tiny blade he took off Tan Man left a blurred arc through the air.

Into the side of Owens' neck.

Frank sighted over the lump of Preston's body. Fired into the shape of a man standing outside. He couldn't tell how good his aim was, kept firing as Owens fell back with his hand slapped over the gushing neck wound.

Eyes and mouth as wide as they could go.

Carmen rolled toward Frank. Threw herself on top of him as Owens opened fire into the back of the van. Sparks and impact. A scorching burn along Frank's ribs.

Carmen screamed into his ear as Owens fell back into the arms of the last man standing.

Frank's final round went over both of their heads. Hit the wall with a burst of concrete chips and dust.

He worked his way out from Carmen's clinging embrace. Stood up on his knees. Pointed the useless pistol at the opening. Distant lights spread Owens' shadow on the wall. Hunched over. Supported by his accomplice.

Their shadows grew as they ran away, and Frank turned to see them stop next to a waiting car. The fourth man got out to help Owens in as the third man ran around to the other side.

Carmen rose up to block his view as she climbed into the driver's seat. Gunned the engine and dropped it in gear. Frank barely had time to grab the edge of the seat before she hit the gas.

He felt like Superman as the acceleration threw him out straight. Gravel spattered the wall behind them like machine gun fire.

As they tore out of the parking lot, Frank saw the gathering by the path heading to the beach. All the kids from Partridge. The university. The locals that always joined them. For some reason, it eased his mind, but he still felt guilty that he couldn't say goodbye.

Chapter Thirty

"Turn left at the end of the bushes!" Stan shouted, hands overhead, clinging to the passenger seat frame as they bounced into the road.

Frank looked back just as the left door slammed shut in the squealing turn. Right into Preston's face as he slid into it. A crunching explosion of blood, and his body rolled to the other side as the van straightened out.

"Did you fucking hear me?" Stan screamed.

"Yes, I fucking heard you!" Carmen screamed back. "Hang on!"

It felt like the van was tipping over as they careened into a narrow gravel drive. Preston flopped through the other door. Hit the pavement and bounced into the oncoming lane.

Not much traffic this late. If he survived the door to the face and the tumble onto the street, maybe he wouldn't get plowed by a car. But hopefully he *would*.

"Where the fuck am I going?" Carmen shouted.

Stan looked up like he was going to be able to see from

his angle. "To the brown garage. Around the right side to the carport in back."

A bump sent Frank off his knees again. Crashing down on his belly. His vision grayed. Particles swam at the edges. He felt his fingers slipping.

Carmen slowed to take the corner at the garage with less speed than her last two turns. Frank tried to keep himself from landing on Stan, but his fingers were done.

Stan cried out when he hit him. Frank scrambled to keep away from the injured leg. Ended up digging his fists into Stan's side.

Carmen hit the brakes at the back of the building, and Frank rolled up Stan's body to smash into the back of the center console.

It seemed like ten minutes passed as they did nothing but listen to each other pant and moan.

Carmen killed the engine. Lifted a shaking hand to point out the window. "There's another van."

Frank got to his knees. Squinted through his good eye to see a brown Dodge parked under a metal roof. An old conversion van with side steps and matching curtains.

"The keys are in the glovebox," Stan said.

Carmen swallowed. "Get the money."

Frank looked around the floor in the back of the van. "What money?"

She leaned her head back. "It's in the center console. Twenty-five thousand in cash. Smuggling."

Frank almost asked what they had been smuggling. Then he realized it was at least alligators. Not sex slaves, but exotic animals. He wondered what else was in the bags back in the garage.

He bent over to release the latch. Found the money in wrapped stacks inside a Provisions bag. Slid on his ass through the layer of blood to the open door. Fell down to his feet like it was the first time he'd stood on his own in a month.

He jogged over to the other van. Opened the passenger door to throw the money onto the floor. Got the keys from the glovebox. Frank caught his reflection in the window glass before shutting the door. A translucent zombie head floating on his shoulders.

He slammed it and hustled to the driver's side. Reached in to fit the key and start the engine. He turned back to the white van in confusion. Wondered why nobody had followed him.

He almost slapped his forehead. Stan *couldn't* follow. Halfway to the open doors in the back, he paused.

Why hadn't Carmen come out?

He shifted direction to run to her door. Threw it open. Looked down in horror at the blood soaking through her shirt. Filling her lap. Dripping from the side of the seat.

"No, no, no …" The only words he could think of. A repetitive mantra that rose in pitch and frequency as he took her into his arms. Her head lolled against his shoulder. Her blood made a warm trail down the fronts of his thighs.

Frank nearly dropped her when he felt her breath on his neck. Hiked her up higher in his arms and carried her to the other van. Got the door open. Heaved her into the plush passenger's seat. She groaned, and her eyes opened.

Carmen's unfocused gaze drifted down to his face. She blinked. Saw him. Smiled. Reached out to him, and he took her fingers in his. Brought them to his lips.

"I've never had a man." She shook her head and swallowed. And her voice was a whisper he could barely hear over the rumble of the van's V-8 when she continued. *"I've never had anybody make me feel the way you did."*

"No, no, no …" Frank pressed her hand into his throbbing cheek.

"It was the first time in my life I felt like something."

Her fingers loosened in his. She looked away. Settled back in the seat. "Something that mattered."

Another woman suffering because of him.

"Thank you," she breathed.

What had he done that was so special? He wasn't worth this.

He wasn't worth anything.

Her eyes closed, and for a frozen moment, Frank thought she had died. But he could see her chest rise and fall with her breath. Just a flutter. But for now, that was enough.

He put her hand in her lap. Eased the door shut. Limped back to the white van. Pain blossomed in every joint. Every limb. In his head. Like the excitement had made him forget about it for a time.

He got to the back to find Stan sitting with his legs dangling off the bumper, elbows on his knees. Panting as a line of drool stretched down from his lips to his lap.

Frank wasted no time getting his shoulder up under Stan's armpit. Pulled him up, and he wasn't sure who groaned louder.

It was slow hopping progress to the van. Into the wide side door where Stan pushed himself in to roll over and cover his eyes with his arms.

Frank closed the doors and rushed to the driver's door. Tried three times before he could successfully climb up into the seat. He paused to catch his breath. Leaned over to put his hand on Carmen's shoulder. "I think we're gonna make it."

She slumped to the side at his touch. Her wild red hair

cushioned her face as her head hit the window. Her eyes were open staring slits.

He didn't need to check. Frank knew she was dead.

"The lane continues back into the trees for an eighth of a mile," Stan said. "Once at the end, just turn right. Go south for a couple hours. Piece of cake. Unless we get stopped or you pass out or something."

Frank pulled his hand back into his lap. "Worry about yourself. I'm just fine."

He followed Stan's directions, and soon enough, they were heading south. No pursuit. No hurry. Just a family out for a nice overnight drive.

The trickle of blood rolling down his side felt no different than the tears dripping into his beard.

Stan's muttered directions from the floor got them just outside of Ocala before they needed to stop for gas. Frank's eye was burning. Swollen and full of grit. A couple of hours ago, he'd told Stan he needed to pee. Stan had told him to just go with it. Hunched over the steering wheel like an old lady who couldn't see in the dark, and he had refused. Tightened up until they got where they were going. Or to a gas station.

The sun was just starting to brighten the sky. Every once in a while, it would shine through the distant trees. Into the cab to blind his good eye. Then to glitter in Carmen's hair.

He took an exit that promised a handful of gas stations. Went three intersections down before pulling into a Willie's. Next to a pump as far away from the building as possible. Right next to a kid wearing a hoodie gassing up a cream-colored Cutlass.

Frank reached into the floor. Past Carmen's cooling knee. Grabbed a bag of cash.

"I don't fucking like this," Stan croaked.

"Choice do we got? Shoulda left it with a full tank. You want me to pee in it?"

"I just don't like it."

Frank took a thousand dollars. Slid out of the driver's seat. He had to hang on to keep his knees from buckling and dumping him on the ground.

The kid was facing away. Putting his gas cap back on. Frank held up the money and cleared his throat. "Excuse me."

The kid turned around without suspicion. Just a mild curiosity. He saw Frank's face. Jerked back in shock. Saw the money. Froze as his shock deepened.

Frank turned his head to keep the good side showing. "Five hundred bucks to fill up my tank. Another five hundred bucks to forget you ever saw me."

The kid's eyebrows rose up to meet the bottom edge of the hood hanging over his forehead. "Man, the only time I see a face like that is in my nightmares."

He snatched the money so fast, Frank wouldn't have been able to stop him on his best day. The kid shook his head. Kept Frank in the corner of his eye as he stretched the hose to the fuel door. Slid the money in his pocket as he filled the tank.

Once finished, he dropped the dispenser back into its hook. "You have a blessed day."

He got into his own car without putting Frank's gas cap back on. Frank sighed as he threaded between the Dodge and the pump. Put it back on himself.

He pulled out into a stream of sunlight that baked the side of his face. Listened to Stan snore for a few minutes before waking him up for the next set of directions.

Frank realized he forgot to find a restroom a mile in. As his laughter brought fresh beats of pain radiating through his head, he took Stan's advice from before. Peed right in his seat.

The shame was smothered by relief, and for a while, he thought of nothing but the sunlight hitting the other cars. Shining through the trees. Playing in the shadows of the Spanish moss hanging over the roads in Wildwood.

Reflecting off the copper roof of the house Stan told him to pull up to. A narrow driveway edged in volcanic rock.

He wasn't completely stopped when the front door swung open, and a huge black man stomped out with a shotgun held up in front of him.

Frank was sure he knew him, but he stared at the man's angry face, unable to figure out who it was. He watched the man move down the porch steps to the driver's side of the van.

Frank saw the man's mouth snarling words. He lowered the window to catch most of it.

"—that shit in reverse, and drive right on outta here, motherfucker!"

Frank raised his hands. Shrugged before dropping them into his lap. Put his head back.

"Frank?" the man said.

Frank smiled as he finally recognized Mo's voice. He relaxed. They made it.

"My God, Frank. What happened?"

Mo's voice rose into a shout, but Frank didn't bother trying to figure out what he was saying. The words weren't meant for him.

He was done.

Chapter Thirty-One

FRANK WOKE to throbbing pain and an unyielding stiffness. A head full of pressure. A strip of light burning into the room from a gap in the curtains.

He turned with a wince. A hiss drawn through clenched teeth. He worked his feet out from under the damp sheets. Held on to the bed as the room swung away from him. Got to a seated position where he sat as tall as he could until the pain sank back down, and the vertigo stopped tightening his throat.

He looked around. Dark paneling. White trim. An open door leading to a bathroom.

He put his hands out in front of him for balance as he stood and stumbled toward the toilet. His right hand was wrapped in an ace bandage from his knuckles to just past his wrist.

The air burned across his sweaty skin. His teeth chattered together every time he exhaled.

He made it into the bathroom. Avoided looking at the mirror as he used the side of the bathtub for support. He didn't trust himself to do his business standing. Sat on the ring with a sigh. Elbows on his knees. Head hanging down.

There was a wide bandage over his left hip. A slight red dampness in the center. Bruised skin around the edges. He tried to think back to when that injury happened. Couldn't quite place it in the blur of memory from inside the back of the white van.

Instead, he got flashes of somebody holding him up as he walked into the cool interior of the house. Hands peeling his clothes off. He wondered if it had been Mo or Gen.

It didn't matter.

Where was Stan? What had they done with Carmen's body?

Questions he didn't want to answer right now.

How long had he been here?

It took him two attempts to get to his feet. He walked to the sink. Ran the water while looking into the basin. Cupped his hands full. Brought it up to wet his face. Gently exploring his swollen features. The heat around his right eye. The pain across the bridge of his nose.

Frank braced himself before finally looking up.

The blackened slit showed a narrow strip of bloodshot eye peering out. A crusty slice through the eyebrow held shut by neat adhesive strips.

The crooked dent in his nose over a bulbous red mound of angry tissue. He attempted a small breath with his mouth closed. It was like trying to drink through a clogged straw.

He pulled his upper lip back. Still had all his teeth.

Stuck his tongue out to see the tip puffy and red. Small ridges of white skin around the tooth marks.

He ran his fingers over his scalp. Looked up at the

bristle of white stubble. Maybe a couple days' worth of growth.

He flicked the rest of the water from his fingers. Left the bathroom to go back to the bed. Pulled the sheet off to wrap around his shoulders. Held it closed as he shuffled to the door.

Frank parted the door, slowly as possible, pausing in the widening gap as music floated in. A relaxing drone of harmonies over a slow hip-hop beat. Soothing and stimulating.

He liked the instant comfort of it.

Kitchen noises were underneath. Quiet voices. One a deep rumble, the other much higher.

He closed his eyes for a calming breath. Squared his shoulders and walked out into the bright hallway. Down to where it opened into the home's main space. Living room, dining room, and kitchen all in one.

Gen stood at a broad island. The light coming through the window over the sink made her hair look like a golden glow. A cutting board covered in strawberries in front of her.

Mo stood next to her. Putting the cut berries into small baggies. They rocked in time with the music. Both of them smiling. A bitter joy welled up in him. Frank sniffed and swallowed. Then cleared his throat as he intruded on their moment.

Frank didn't want to see what he couldn't have.

They looked up as one, and he was relieved to see no blame on their faces. No anger or hatred. Only open smiles of anticipation.

Gen dropped her knife. Dried her hands on a pink flamingo towel as she rushed around the island. Hit with more force than was probably safe, but he held against it as she threw her arms around him. Put her face against his chest.

"We were so worried about you," she said.

Frank couldn't return her embrace without dropping his sheet. Not the best way to reunite with old friends. So he submitted himself and waited for her to be done.

At least he wasn't crying. He didn't even feel his chest tightening. The weight he always felt just before he let loose. Just a slight resentment at her touch he couldn't explain.

Maybe he'd never cry again. Wouldn't that be something?

Gen pulled back to look up at his face. Stared into his eyes. Her expression drifted into worry, but she simply nodded instead of addressing the expression. Like confirming a suspicion.

Frank noticed that she had lost some of her mass. Her body had leaned out a little. Like she'd hardened. "You look good."

She smiled. "It's good to have you here."

Didn't say *he* looked good, but he couldn't blame her.

"My man," Mo said, his shadow blocking the light from their kitchen window.

Frank was surprised by his appearance. This close made the change shocking. He had lost every scrap of fat from his frame, leaving only chiseled muscle behind. Making his face look hollow. Like a death mask.

Frank tried to work his hand out from under the sheet for a proper greeting, but Mo beat him with a hug that wasn't as crushing as he remembered. Probably mindful of Frank's condition.

Even as tears fell from their eyes, Frank's remained dry. As much as he wanted to join their moment, there were things he needed to know.

"How long have I been here?"

Gen glanced at Mo before spinning back to the kitchen and resuming her position behind the island.

"This is the third day," Mo said.

"Where's Stan?"

"He's good."

"That's not what I asked."

"I know, but I ain't gonna answer. He's somewhere to get care for that leg. Even *we* don't know where. He'll come back around when things cool off."

Frank nodded. "What about Carmen?"

Mo put his hand on Frank's shoulder. "You wanna eat something? Maybe ease into this shit? Or you need to do this right now?"

"It's been three days to you, but to me, I fell asleep with her dead in the passenger seat of the van, then woke up in bed. Like the space between heartbeats. Yes, I need this now."

Mo held his gaze, and though there was a time Frank would have looked away first, this time he waited for Mo to break eye contact.

"Okay," Mo said. "Let's go."

He took Frank's shoulder. Led him to a side door that opened up on a brown lawn. Sunshine hit him like the light had actual weight.

Van scanned the whole yard. An orange RV next to a garage. A pole barn in the back corner of the lot. "What happened to the van?"

"It's in the shed. Took the front seats out for a cleaning. Otherwise, it's pretty straight."

Frank nodded with a grunt. "And Carmen?"

Mo turned him to face the rear of the property. About three acres lined by tall trees. He pointed, but Frank couldn't make out any of the details from that far away. His right eye was still dark and blurry.

"The center fence post."

It took a moment for Frank to realize what he meant. Then he nodded and took an unsteady step.

"You want some shoes or something?" Mo asked.

Frank ignored him. Kept walking. The dry grass was nothing compared to the sharp silica dunes of Playa Dolor.

He pulled the sheet up higher on his shoulders. Tighter around his neck. His sinuses were loosening in the heat. He could smell compost and flowers. His own acrid sweat. Dried blood.

He felt the urge to talk to Sarah. A compulsion so strong, Frank even opened his mouth and took a breath. Then he snapped his teeth shut.

No, he wouldn't burden her with his mistakes any longer.

Besides, something felt wrong about talking to his dead wife while walking to the grave of his dead lover.

A few yards from the fence, Frank saw the soft mound of dirt. He wondered which one of them had dug it. Probably both of them. Together.

There was a concrete cross at the end of the mound. A touch he neither liked nor hated. Just a symbol of death to mark her passing.

Frank stopped with his toes digging into the soft dirt at the bottom. Sighed as he dropped into a crouch. Waited to settle into the soreness in his thighs.

He wanted to talk to her. Tell her the thing he knew she had wanted to hear. Maybe even convince himself that it was true. That he really *had* loved her.

But no … he wouldn't do that. He knew now that gone was *gone*. Sometimes bad things happened, and sometimes there was nothing you could do about it.

Unless you made it through the bad things. Then maybe there *was* something you could do.

Frank thought of Owens. The men like him. The ones he had let get away when he had fallen for the bait. Malick Briar and the easy kill.

Frank *thought* he had lost everything before. But then he had a chance at redemption, only to lose that too. It wasn't just about punishing the men that had wronged his daughter. Or Rory Day. Or the hundreds of other girls that had slipped through the cracks of a terminally broken system. It was about punishing the men that had wronged *him*.

The plan that was forming would never have had room in the head of the man Frank used to be. He truly had nothing left to lose now.

Because how could you lose your soul that you were willing to surrender?

What to read next

Frank Grimm has escaped to Wildwood to recover, but he's still obsessed with revenge. Without his cousin Stan — the only person he was able to trust — his worst impulses run rampant.

Hidden Virtue is the fourth and final book in the *Hidden Justice* series

Get Hidden Virtue today!

A Quick Favor

Thanks for reading *Hidden Shame.*

If you enjoyed this book, please consider writing a review of it on your favorite bookselling site so other readers can enjoy it too. Just a couple of sentences would mean a lot to me.

Thank you!

Nolon & Dave

About the Authors

Nolon King writes fast-paced psychological thrillers set in the glitzy world of entertainment's power players with a bold, insightful voice. He's not afraid to explore the darker side of human nature through stories featuring families torn apart by secrets and lies.

Nolon loves to write about big questions and moral quandaries. How far would you go to cover up an honest mistake? Would you destroy your career to protect your family? How much of your soul would you sell to get the life of your dreams? Would you cheat on your husband to keep your children safe? Would you give in to a stalker's demands to save your marriage?

David W. Wright is the co-author of edge-of-your-seat thrillers including the best-selling post-apocalyptic series *Yesterday's Gone*, the paranoid sci-fi *WhiteSpace* series, and the vigilante series, *No Justice*, as well as standalone thrillers *12*, and *Crash* which was recently optioned for a movie.

David is an accomplished, though intermittent, cartoonist who lives in [LOCATION REDACTED] with his wife and son [NAMES REDACTED.]

He is not at all paranoid.

He is "the grumpy one" on *The Story Studio Podcast* with fellow Sterling and Stone founders, Sean Platt and Johnny B. Truant.

You can email him at david@sterlingandstone.net

We swear, he almost never bites. Unless you feed him after midnight.

Also By Nolon King

Hidden Justice

Hidden Justice

Hidden Honor

Hidden Shame

Hidden Virtue

No Justice

No Justice

No Escape

No Hope

No Return

No Stopping

No Fear

Once Upon A Crime

Once Upon A Crime

Twice Upon A Lie

Three Times a Murder

Dead For Good

Dead For Good

Left For Dead

Dead Of Night

Wake The Dead

Dead For Life

Stand Alone Novels

Pretty Killer

12

Blown

Miserable Lies

The Target

Secrets We Keep

Close To Home

Heat To Obsession

A Simple Kill

Tell Me No Lies

Red Carpet Black

Fade To Black

Victim

Also By David W. Wright

Hidden Justice

Hidden Justice

Hidden Honor

Hidden Shame

Hidden Virtue

No Justice

No Justice

No Escape

No Hope

No Return

No Stopping

No Fear

Karma Police

Jumper

Karma Police

The Collectors

Deviant

The Fall

Homecoming

Yesterday's Gone

October's Gone

Yesterday's Gone Season One

Yesterday's Gone Season Two

Yesterday's Gone Season Three

Yesterday's Gone Season Four

Yesterday's Gone Season Five

Yesterday's Gone Season Six

Tomorrow's Gone

Tomorrow's Gone Season One

Tomorrow's Gone Season Two

Tomorrow's Gone Season Three

Available Darkness

Darkness Itself

Available Darkness Book One

Available Darkness Book Two

Available Darkness Book Three

WhiteSpace

WhiteSpace Season One

WhiteSpace Season Two

WhiteSpace Season Three

Stand Alone Novels

12

Crash

Emily's List

Threshold